Devil's Harvest
Blood Bonds

Written by

Oliver W. Decay

Edited by

Family Decay

This is a work of fiction. All characters, organizations, and events portrayed in this novel are either products of the authors' imagination or are used fictitiously.

linktr.ee/Purple_Mage_Publishing

ISBN 979-8-9927914-3-3

First Edition: March 2025

This book is written under the watchful gaze of Metatromis.

"..."= Means a person is speaking
"{...}"= Means someone is thinking
"[...]"= Means someone is broadcasting their voice

I was crazy once
They locked me in a room   = This is for the others in
A rubber room with a Bat   the chapters main focus.
Bats make me crazy

This is for the main =   I was crazy once
focus of the chapter.   They locked me in a room
                 A rubber room with a Nat
                 Nats make me crazy

I was crazy once
They locked me in a room
A rubber room with a cat
Cats make me crazy
=
This is for all in the chapter.

Prologue
Broken

The sweet smell of lavender fills the air, as gentle buzzing echoes across pale blue walls. The drapes part silently, allowing the dim gray evening sky to spill into the room. Gray hues wash over dark blue sheets, resembling deep, mysterious seas. But there is nothing mysterious about the man lying there.

"{Why did I stay up so late last night?}"

His gaze drifting to the foot of the bed where three empty wine bottles sit. Clenching the sheets in frustration before finally letting go to silence the alarm that has been blaring for ten minutes.

"SIGH!"

Running his hands through his hair and down his face,
"{I should really take a shower. Maybe even shave. Can't stay in this moment. Push through... just go past it.}"

Gaining the courage to finally move, he stumbles toward the bathroom.

"Damn wine still lingering," his words hiss.

"{Guess sobering up is the first order of business before seeing the doctor.}"

In front of the mirror-less sink, he pauses, running his left hand over his unshaven face.

"{The doctor would probably forgive a little stubble,}"

"{I could just say I had a rough morning... no. Then he'd start asking questions. Better to just say I forgot.}"

Dragging his feet to the shower, his eyes stay fixed on the faucet. He grabs a metal pole hidden behind the toilet and uses it to twist the shower knob. Water bursts out, forcing him to step back. He waits a moment, cautiously holding the pole under the stream to test it. Nothing happens.

Sigh

Gripping the metal handrail beside the shower, he steps in slowly, one foot at a time. His arm reaches out instinctively to balance himself. It's been a long time since he's had a proper shower. He struggles to wash himself as his left hand braced the handrail and the other is forced to lather up his loofah. He tries to keep his head out of the water as much as possible, but then he slips. The stream of water hits his face, his grip tightens desperately around the handrail. His thoughts race as he fights to steady himself.

"{Out of the moment. Out! Of! The! Moment!}"

...*KKKKSSSSHSHSHSHSHSH.. BANG!*

It's not enough. Ripping the handrail from the wall, he tumbles backward, dragging the shower curtain with him. Steam clouds the air as he scrambles to shut off the water, slamming the knob with the metal pole.

Pg.2

Now drenched, he collapses onto the bathroom floor. Water pools around him as he crawls into the corner, his breathing ragged. Shaking as he laid there, he wished only to *fade* from this world.

Chapter 1
Drake

Icy rain pounded the shattered city, pooling in torn-up streets and overflowing from clogged drains. The deluge streaked far below a fogged window in a crumbling apartment loft, where the steady thump of a punk band rattled the walls from below.

Felicity stood from the decrepit mattress she had spent the night wishing to leave, her blonde curls falling over her eyes. Restless, she moved through the decay of her loft, a cracked ceiling with a steady drip that added to the cacophony. The broken blinds that barely cover a single window turned to iron bars; the chains of this monstrous city hold her tight.

Sigh

Rubbing her eyes as the floorboards creaked beneath her. Felicity pushed through the piles of trash; pulling out a small, tarnished kettle. Filling it with gray water from a leaking tap, she reached into the cabinet over the stove. Finding a box of matches to see that only one had remained. Nervously, she struck it. The bulb snapped, and the match crumbled in her fingers.

Her frustration boiled over. She kicked and yanked at the knobs on the stove, anger filling her like an open flame. Over and over again, she twisted & muttered faint words until a loud snap echoed from the stove.

Fire burst forth from all four burners, panic replacing her rage. Scrambling to turn the broken knobs, she steadied her breathing.

Quickly, she extinguished the flames on three of the four burners. Leaving the last one on, she set the kettle down exhaling sharply. Glancing back at the man sprawled across her sheets.

"Oi!"
She barked, grabbing a dirty fork from the sink and tossing it at him.

He grumbled under the stained comforter, his muddy black hair just visible.

"Aaahhhnnmhhmm..."
"Wake up dimwit!"

Storming over, she ripped the blanket away, revealing his heavy frame and deep scars. Yanking him upright, she grabbed the remote and turned on the ancient TV in the corner. Static buzzed before the screen lit up in harsh gray and white light.

"If we're late to meet my brothers again, we'll lose the work,"

She snapped, locking her eyes on him as she moved back toward the kettle.

"Don't screw up tonight's plans with your hungover sleep."

He sighed and finally stood, the light from the TV casting shadows over his broad shoulders. Standing at seven foot three, Drake was anything if not a mountain of a man. From a pile of dirty clothes near the bed, he pulled on ripped black jeans, and a security uniform shirt that stretched tight against his rugged arms.

"Don't get your stockings in a twist, Felicity. They're a pair of knights. Helping their less-off sister is the least they can do to feel high and mighty."

She rolled her eyes, wiping down two dirty mugs with her shirt. Dropping small cloth bags of coffee into each, she poured boiling water over them, handing him a mug. He gulped the drink in one go, bag and all, then handed it back.

"Eeck! What the heck, Drake!"

She exclaimed while wrinkling her nose. "That's disgusting! You shouldn't eat the coffee bags."

He grinned, opening his mouth to show her. "I'm not eating it. Just savoring the flavor."

She shook her head, sticking her tongue out. "Still gross."

Shshshshshsh... click...

The static flickered to a deep crimson-and-gold LNBS logo, accompanied by jazzy intro music. A polished man in a sleek eggplant suit, his jet-black hair gleaming under studio lights, sat beside a pale woman with sharp features and striking feline like crimson eyes.
"Good morning citizens of Lexington."

Speaking in a soft welcoming tone,
"It's one dastardly cold fall morning, wouldn't you agree, dear?"

The man chuckled,
"Oh dearie, you're absolutely right."

Their harmonious laughter filled the air before she continued.

"Hopefully, you're snuggled up with a cozy blanket and a mug of black cherry coffee to start your day."

The male news anchor raised his LNBS-branded mug with a shining smile,
"Aah, isn't it delicious? Grab yourself a cup at your local market today."

The camera zoomed in on the female news anchor. Her gaze directed to the viewers,
"Due to the bad weather, folks are advised to stay indoors. But only after they enjoy the Fall Harvest Festival held here in downtown Lexington."

"Treat yourself to a candied golden apple or a spicy ruby ale! And don't forget, curfew tonight is 8 p.m. for the Howling Blood Moon."

The male news anchor's tone grew sharp as he addressed the viewers,
"That's right. On nights like this, crime rates triple. Reports of missing persons spike, often leading to dead ends. Stay safe folks."

The broadcast ended with a commercial for cherry petal wine before Drake clicked the TV off. Tossing the remote onto the bed Drake leaned back, his dark blue eyes tracing Felicity's form under an oversized Core-Toss jersey. She caught his gaze, raising a questioning eyebrow as he opened his mouth to speak but said nothing, as instead his mind filled with the memories of his little brother.

"{I thought I'd have a bit more time to talk to him before this.}"

Drakes gaze pushing away at the ceiling, now watching the slow drip from the crack above. "Why do we have to do this tonight? Why not tomorrow or any other time?"

Scoffing, she finished her coffee with a smirk. In a flash she bent over pinching his side,
"What's the matter, big Bear? Afraid of some boogeyman coming to get you in the dark?"

Drake grabbed her hand, pulling it close,
"If it's you bumping in the night, I wouldn't mind."

She snorted, tossing the hot coffee bag at his face,
"Keep it to yourself for tonight."

Changing into her security uniform, her voice turned serious,
"Tonight has to go perfectly if we're getting out of this mess. Lincoln and Anthony will be on to you and your brother. Lincoln's already run your background checks. You're lucky Ethan's came up clean but I vouched for you, so don't screw this up. Lincoln's no softy like Anthony. He'll try to get under your skin. Just keep quiet and do your job."

Drake wiped the coffee water from his face as he tossed the other coffee bag into his mouth,
"Yeah, I got it."

Leaving the decaying loft they descended the 56 flights of rain slick stairs. Drake leaned over the railing, spitting out the two coffee bag remnants. Reaching the ground floor, the two slipped into the alley where a bulky black SUV idled belching black smoke. Climbing in, they slammed the doors shut. The engine sputtered to life, roaring off into the night.

Chapter 2
Ethan

Drip... drip... drip.

Tiny drops of gray sludge fell from cracks in the aluminum roof, caused by the pitter patter of rain outside. Landing on Ethan's cheek as he slept in a nest of sleeping bags. The drops pooled until they ran down into his mouth.

"ACK! PFFT! Gra-Gra-GROSS!"

He sat up instantly, spitting out the slimy water. His eyes darted around the cluttered room, filled with piles of electronics and broken gadgets, until he spotted a bottle of murky brown water. Taking a swig to rinse out his mouth.

"{Ugh... The water didn't look that murky when I found it last night. Maybe that Yoba fruit can help out that milky water after taste. I can even sneak in some commercials since I woke up earlier than I wanted.}"

Stretching and shaking off the morning grogginess. He claps his hands in a cheer.
"Heck-heck- Heck Yeah!"

Ethan wiggled his thin frame through the maze of parts and junk, heading to a cluttered shelf in the back.
"{Aw, crap! I forgot to pack some of my bots for today.}"

Turning back to his sleeping bag cocoon, he grabbed a battered black backpack, retracing his steps back to the shelf displaying his creations.

"{Hmm...}"

He scanned the rows of small robotic creatures.

"Which- which baby wa- want- wants to come to work with daddy?"

The shelf was packed with an assortment of robots that resembled different animals. There were fish, birds, insects, reptiles, and even a few mammals. Each bot seemed to be built for a specific purpose.

"Oh jeez, don't-don't-don't all volunteer at-at... once."

Ethan stammered with a laugh as he loaded a few into his bag. Reaching for a large black case, he pulled out several small glass bottles filled with a squirming liquid.

"{I hope I don't need these, but you never know what a vault's going to throw at you}"

Looking around as if he forgot something, "{Oh yeah!}"

Tossing a few bottles into his bag, Ethan leaped, diving over stacks of papers and metal boxes. He slid to a stop near a tattered brown bag, pulling out a cobalt crystal wristband. Sliding it onto his right wrist, the band glowed a deep blue light around it's rims. Vibrating, it shrank to fit snugly around his wrist.

"COMMAND CODE: BADGER!"

A white screen projected from the band, and a honey badger emerged from a series of digital holes. The creature bit at the screens text, replacing the redacted username with Ethan's name.

He patted the wristband as he spoke to it, "Nice job, li-li-little buddy,"

Ethan tossed the brown bag aside and wandered back to the middle of the room. Rubbing his stomach, he raised a finger. "{Oh yeah, that yoba fruit.}"

He made his way back to his robotic zoo of a shelf. Shifting some bots aside to find his over ripened prized. As soon as he grabbed it, a swarm of fruit flies buzzed into the air.

"AW, ka-ka-COME ON!" Ethan yelled, swatting at the pests with one hand while clutching the fruit in the other. His stutter worsened as frustration took hold.

"This-this-this is mine! I ba-ba-ba bought... it fair an-an-an-and square!"

Seeing that it's not enough, he leaned over, picking up one of his robots that resembled a skunk. Lifting the tail he yanked it back to spray the flies with a horrific smelly odor.

"HA AHA HA, Ta-ta-take that nasties!!"

Agitated, he rushed to a table at the back of the room, hoping the flies wouldn't follow through the skunk's spray. Grabbing a small knife, he sliced the fruit, carefully salvaging the few edible pieces.

Chop! Squish! Chop-Chop!

He scraped the intact bits into a bowl, plopping down in front of a DIY television he had built. Calming himself with a deep breath.

Click! Click-click-click.

Rolling one of the balls of yoba with his fingers he flicks a knob and spins a small dial to turn on the tv. Clicking a pedal he surfs through tv shows, stopping when he comes across a commercial he has seen before. A flash of white light fills the small cubby space he calls home. Beams of red, blue, and green flash vibrantly as the image on the screen magnify to fit the full screen. A colorful ad about moist and fluffy cakes play out.

"Their creamy white filling is enriched with tangy orange cream soda that will leave your taste buds in the graces of elegance. Go to your local grocer to find Sir Tang's Moncha Cakes."

The screen shows a well-dressed couple being served the cakes. The butler, dressed in a bright orange & white suit, sneaks one for himself. The three of them take one bite in unison. As the orange cream filling hits their tongues it caused each of them to overact the feelings of joy. The screen darkens to a logo of an older pale woman wearing a heavy white sun dress. She pulls the name Granny Charm's Goodies from an oven out of shot of the screen. A small tag reads at the bottom of the plate in ridiculously small texts.

-Ingredients may vary-

"{Haha ingredients may vary; that's why Drake found a rat in one and mom told him better luck next time.}"
"AHA HA HA HA!!"

Click

"Long day watching the kids? Dreadful day at work that just wouldn't end fast enough? Well than I have the answer for that. Pink petal Wine. A sweet & sensual wine that is gentle like the cherry petals that fall from the trees it's harvested from."

A man sits at a stunning dark cherrywood table. Taking a bottle of a fine pink liquid, he pours it into a small pearl wine glass.

Fingering the glasses fine rose petal edges, he looks seductively into the camera,
"When you want to take a moment and make it about yourself, when you're unsure but know you want a sweet treat to keep you wanting more. Come grab from the vines of your heart. We gently gather each rose cherry, so we can bring you our best."

The man runs his left hand through his hair. Taking a deep sip from the wine glass the camera pans out as a title forms over his image.

"Pink petal Wine, one of the top ten wines in Red Barrels Fall collection."

Ethan groaned,
"{I don't even drink, but I know that's gotta be overpriced.}"
Click.
The LNBS logo flickered onto the screen, followed by a peppy host with makeup plastered onto her face.
"Good morning, Lexington! It's 6 a.m., and where are your glasses?" she chirped. "I'm Caroline Addison-Tate, and here's your *Sunny Smiles Morning News!*"

Pg.14

She leaned closer to the camera, her tone turning sinister,
"Ladies, take a sip. I've got some startling news to start the day. The Bishop Stone Museum of Historic Arts and Technology burned down last night. What appeared to be a simple robbery turned into an act of terrorism."

Ethan froze, his sticky fingers hovering over a ball of yoba as he staired out at the screen.

"Pearl Officers say the perpetrators used military-grade firearms and explosives to hold off SWAT teams while they planted charges on the museum's main structure. The only items recovered were a few bird-like drones used by the terrorists, and a backpack locked in the primary vault. Police are already at work hacking the salvageable memory drives from the drones."

Caroline took a sip from a glass of pink wine before flashing a strained smile.

"In lighter news, a rain and lightning advisory has been issued. Those in low altitudes should find their local Key-approved flood shelter. Stay safe-"

Click.

The screen went dark, blanketing the room in silence. Ethan leaned back, finishing the last piece of yoba. It's sweet meaty taste lingering in his thoughts, before he was forced out from his bliss.

"{Crap! Guess I *really* have to do this job for Drake now. Let's just hope he doesn't cheat me out of my share again. I've got a vacation to plan, and a father to find. Goodbye you lousy island!}"

Chapter 3
Lincoln

Chiiiii... chig chig chig... click.

A set of keys rattled in heavy hands as they slid into the ignition.

Vva vaahh viiin... vvviiinn... boom-chunk-boooom.

The engine sputtered and groaned before roaring to life. Rainwater rushed down the cracked dark charcoal tires and pealing chrome-plated steel rims. Windows open slightly to release the stifling heat from an overworked car heater.

The radio hummed to life, cutting through the awkward silence and the steady pitter patter of rain on the windshield. A proud masculine voice blended with an elegant, flowing feminine one, the two together filled the SUV's cab.

Clearing their throat, the masculine voice laughed lightly before speaking,
"Thanks Bruce, for that detailed Core Toss Match line-up. For those just tuning in, a Dangerous Weather Advisory is in place for Mou Yoba, Berryton, and Tinvilla. Residents of these districts are urged to stay indoors. Major highways connecting these areas are now closed due to flooding from the hurricane off Bravati's southwestern coast. However, capital cities like Lexington and Berry City are still holding their Harvest Day festivals."

The feminine voice followed smoothly, "It's hoped the storm will weaken before reaching them. Still, police have locked down city gates to prevent traffic in case of severe flooding. Residents in low-lying areas should immediately head to their nearest Key Flood Shelter. Please call *69 to connect with an operator for check-in locations. Volunteers will continue staffing shelters and hospitals for those stranded."

After a brief silence, the masculine voice coughed and continued, "In financial news, International Key Sales Stocks are up 12%, possibly due to the buyout of Caster Net Corp Communications(CNCC). The merging Key Broadcasting Communications Company(KBCC) has reassured users that Net Bands will stay operational through the transition. Older models will receive updates, but those experiencing connection issues are advised to contact KBCC Helplines for assistance. Stay tuned after our sponsor break for updates on the Bishop Stone Museum bombing."

Click...

Lincoln shut the radio off. He glanced at Drake's reflection in the rearview mirror but quickly returned his attention to the road ahead. "{As if I thought this job wouldn't be easy to begin with. She had to bring along another street rat that is hurt and in need of a home. Add on the discharge and I would have just thought of him as dirt. Good to know it's traitorous dirt. Damn storm just adds to everything.}"

"The news is right, you two,"
Lincoln said flatly, cutting in from his racing
thoughts.

"The storm's going to hammer us all night.
Visibility will be low, and power outages are likely.
Radio in any incidents to me before taking action."

Anthony leaned back with a grin.
"Yeah, but we'll all be stuck in shelters anyway. No
big deal. If there's a power outage, Felicity can just
reset the main breaker at the clubhouse."

Lincoln's gaze darkened, cutting sharply toward
Anthony.

"Keep your c-net bands at full volume. Check in
every hour, on the hour. If you take a break, radio it
in and note everything in your logs. If you need the
restroom, buzz the call-in, but otherwise, stay sharp
and stick to protocol."

Felicity, sitting in the back passenger seat, turned to
glare at Lincoln through the misty rearview mirror.

"What's your problem? Most residents are away or
locked up in their homes for the holiday. The techs
won't even start work until morning. Why don't
you ease off?"

Anthony cleared his throat awkwardly, trying to
diffuse the tension,
"ACK HEM!! Well, both Lincoln and I served during
the Mou Yoba Incident, Nice to know there's
another vet here."

Felicity's voice turned cold,
"No one forced you two to do anything after the
bombing."

Pg.18

Anthony smiled nervously at Drake, trying to lighten the mood,
"Well, she's not wrong, but we thought it was the right thing to do."

Drake's expression remained cold and distant, his silence filling the truck's cabin.

Anthony tried again,
"So... how long have you two been together?"

Lincoln shot another glare at Anthony. Drake tried to speak with a sly smile, but Felicity cut in before he could respond,
"We're not *together* like that. We're just friends!"

Lincoln's gaze softened, as Anthony blinked in surprise.
"Oh, I just thought—"

"You thought wrong,"
Felicity snapped.

"I'm just helping him out with his little brother. They're looking for their father, and I figured some quick cash would help. They're leaving as soon as the storm clears."

Drake's jaw tightened, his frustration evident as he leaned against the armrest, staring out at the rain-soaked road.

Anthony leaned back with a sigh,
"Well, I hope you find him, Drake. And from one
vet to another, thanks for your service."

Lincoln chuckled darkly,
"Hah! Thanks for your service? You mean your
dishonorable discharge."

Drake's head snapped up.

Lincoln's laughter faded as his eyes locked with
Drake's in the rearview mirror,
"Yeah, I know about it. Background check says
you're squeaky clean—except for that little
discharge. But why, I wonder?"

Drake's fists clenched tightly. Felicity placed a
calming hand over one of them, but her glare
toward Lincoln was cut short by his icy stare.

The SUV screeched to a halt outside a small
security station. Rain drummed against the
windows as Lincoln leaned closer,
"So why were you discharged, Drake? What's your
story? Heck what service did you do! I was a
surgeon; you know someone saving lives..."

Drake's silence was deafening. His fist trembled,
ready to strike, but a sudden knock at the driver's
window interrupted the tense moment.

A young man stood in the rain, no older than
nineteen, his military-style haircut slick with water.

He smiled brightly,
"Hey, Lincoln! You startled the heck out of me!"

Lincoln rolled down the window, his jaw tight as his fingers drummed impatiently on the steering wheel. His glare snapped to Benny, and the younger man's expression faltered into unease.

Anthony leaned forward, his grin softening the tension,
"You doing okay out here, Benny? You know how grumpy Lincoln gets when he's stuck in a storm."

Benny chuckled nervously, glancing between Anthony and Lincoln,
"Oh, uh, yeah! I'm fine. The rain's a bit of a pain, but it beats last week's power outage. Thanks for asking Anthony."

Anthony smirked and gestured toward the gate switch,
"Think you can open that up for us before Lincoln starts growling at everyone? It's been a long drive."

Benny's eyes widened as he reached for the gate controls,
"Oh, yeah! Sorry about that! Here you go."

As the gate creaked open, Anthony nodded approvingly,
"Good to hear kid. Just keep your head up, storms pass quicker than they feel."

Benny chuckled again, a little less nervous this time,
"Thanks Anthony. Stay safe out there okay?"

Lincoln leaned back, gripping the steering wheel tightly,
"Keep those service windows locked Benny. It's going to get worse tonight, and the last thing we need is another flooded station. Got it?"

Benny replied sheepishly,
"Uhhh... Yes sir!"

Heading back into the station, he locked the windows as the SUV rolled forward into the community.

The main road snaked through, flanked by vibrant red and purple flowers cascading down the sidewalks. Many were uprooted or shredded by the storm, with petals and leaves scattered across the asphalt. Despite their beauty, the vibrant red and purple flowers often struggled to survive in the Bravati's environment anyway. They died frequently, requiring monthly replacements to keep the community's manicured appearance intact.

Finally, the road brought them to the imposing Main Clubhouse. Its height matched that of mountainous buildings back in downtown Lexington. The many windows and pillars lined up to form a shape reminiscent of a monstrous face. The gigantic double entry doors, covered in heavy black iron crowning, cast long shadows resembling jagged teeth. Against the stormy sky, the building loomed lifeless, almost haunted.

Felicity muttered under her breath,
"Let's just hope the wildlife knows to behave tonight."

Anthony handed her a small umbrella,
"You're stationed here with Baillie. Patrol the pools, dining hall, entertainment room, and lobby. Should be an easy night."

Felicity scoffed, snatching the umbrella,
"Yeah, sure. I've got the easy part... Animals."

Slam

Placing the vehicle back into drive, Lincoln shifted into gear turning the wheel, steering the SUV up the eastern rounded road.

"Uuuhhh... hey, Lincoln, I thought I was going to be stationed at my usual post on the north end of the park?"

Lincoln's gaze flicked toward Drake; his expression twisted.
"I thought we'd change things up."

"That way I can keep a closer eye on our new employee tonight, in case he needs help."

Anthony quickly tried to interject,
"Yeah but-"
Lincoln continued, his voice sharp,
"I'm the one who's worked this park the longest, right?"
Anthony hesitated before he spoke,
"Well yeah, but-"

Before Anthony could finish, Lincoln pressed on,
"And *technically* since I'm Team Lead, I can also switch stations. Right?"

Pg.23

"Well yeah. But I don't—"

Lincoln said with a smirk,
"Don't worry about it. Besides, the eastern gate's
pretty easy. Mostly just pet parks and sports fields."

The vehicle misfired as Lincoln pressed the gas,
causing it to lurch slightly.
"Plus, I've got to handle the northern gate to work
on the SUV."

Nodding toward the dashboard.
"You hear that? She's sounding pretty rough."

Lincoln stopped in front of the Eastern Guard
Station. Stepping out of the vehicle, Anthony
turned to look back at Lincoln, shaking his head
before conceding.
"Alright, I'll see you tomorrow morning."

Closing the door, he crossed the empty road. The
SUV roared to life again, picking up speed.
Rounding the clubhouse, Lincoln passed the North
Gate Station, continuing toward the West Gate
Station.

Lincoln's gaze remained locked on Drake's; a white
fiery intensity flickered in his eyes. He leaned
forward slightly, his voice low and commanding
towards Drake.

"I'll say this once, and only once!"

His words turning to a burning ice,
"Don't make me repeat myself! Do you
understand?"

Drake's eyes releasing the beast within, his
expression tense,
"Yes sir!"
Pg.24

Lincoln spoke firmly, each word deliberate and
precise,
"You'll be patrolling Dawn Grove. Everything you
need is in the western shack. The site's still under
construction, so don't mess with anything out
there. Once you're on-site, turn on the cameras and
clock in. The C-Net Band will sync with the shack.
Call me every hour, on the hour. If there's an
incident, you contact me, and only me first! If you
talk back, so help me I'll have you and your brother
removed from this park without pay. I don't care
about your sob story. If you and your brother have
to walk home in the middle of the night in this
storm! Then that'll be your choice, but it'll be your
only choice if you test me. Do I make myself clear?"
"Yes sir!"

"Good dog,"
Lincoln sneered.
"Now get the hell out of my SUV!"

Chapter 4
Benjamin

Rain poured over the glistening silver steel fence that encased the city-sized gated park. Green pine trees swayed in the storm's howling wind. Their branches weighed down by the downpour of the storm. Brightly colored flowers lined the roads leading into the park, their vibrant petals scattered by the relentless rain. At the park's center loomed a hulking mansion-like clubhouse, flanked by pools, tennis courts, and even an 18-hole golf course. The sheer opulence of the community seemed out of place amid the chaos of the storm.

At each entrance to the park's three residential communities and at the main entrance gate, stood a small security station. Each station was equipped with a drab gray guard building, their spotlights cutting faint beams through the downpour. A navy-green moped zipped through the rain, skidding to a stop behind the Southern Guard Station. Its rider, a young man in a bright blue security uniform, dismounted and hurried inside.

"Good morning June," Benjamin called out; his voice cheerful despite the echoes of the storm outside.

Entering the Southern Guard Station, he saw the elderly woman in a matching uniform to his, had dozed off in an office chair. Her head slumped against the desk. The monitors in front of her buzzed softly, displaying live feeds of the park's empty roads and facilities. Benjamin set his rain-soaked jacket and backpack on the table beside her, chuckling softly. Moving to the coffee maker, he filled it with clear water and a dark crimson powder before flipping a few switches. As the machine hissed to life, he slid his blue ID card into the clock-in station in the far back corner of the room. Returning to the coffee maker, he poured the freshly brewed dark cherry coffee into one of the mugs built into the side of the device. Walking back, he gently nudged her shoulder.

June jolted awake with a sharp gasp, causing Benjamin to scream.

"AAAH!"

"AAAH! June, it's me!"

Benjamin exclaimed, holding up his hands to his face. "It's okay, you fell asleep. Your shift's over."

"Oh no, I nodded off again!"

June flustered,
"I'm so sorry, Benny. I'm just no good at 16 hour shifts."

Benjamin smiled softly as he handed her the mug. "It's fine June. Look, why don't I talk to Lincoln about moving me to your shift in the mornings? I can help you out more. Plus now that Drake got hired I can walk away from overnights. He'll understand."

June took the mug, her hands trembling slightly as she blew on the coffee.
"Thanks Benny. You're such a sweet boy. You're going to make someone the luckiest person someday."

Benny blushed, laughing nervously while he rubbed the back of his head.
"Thanks June. But I've got a few things to figure out before I'm ready for that."

June gathered her belongings, picking up a small purple cloth-covered book. It's frayed edges revealed a cover that was made from a strange teal-gray wood. It was hard but still felt flexible.

Benjamin's curiosity got the better of him. "June what's that one about?"

"Oh, it's some kind of fairy tale about a wizard," She handed it over to him.

"I think it's tied to a game some kid made, but it's too complicated for me. If you want, you can borrow it."

Benjamin examined the book, its cover reading *Tales of Purple Roads*. Flipping through, he found no index or summary page, just dense, ornate text. Sliding his ID card into the book's pages as a makeshift bookmark, he set it aside.

"Thanks June. It'll give me something to do tonight."

She smiled warmly before punching out at the clock-in station. Benny watched her disappear into the freezing rain; her figure swallowed by the storm as she waved goodbye. The shack felt colder, and just a bit lonelier now.
Pg.28

Benny glanced around groaning softly. June hadn't cleaned up while she was on shift. "{Great. Just what I needed. If Lincoln shows up and sees this mess, I'm toast.}"

Sighing, he grabbed a rag getting to work. Dusting off surfaces, wiping windows, and finally taking the trash to the compactor outside, he muttered to himself the entire time. Once done, he collapsed into the green leather office chair, rubbing his eyes.

"{Okay, not bad. Maybe now I can actually relax.}"

The monitors in front of him flickered faintly. Most showed dark, rain-blurred images of empty streets and driveways. He leaned forward, adjusting the controls, when the car alert alarm buzzed sharply. A long, dark limousine pulled up to the exit gate. Its matte eggplant paint gleamed under the spotlights, and a distinctive hood ornament; a silver eye covered by a grey hand confirmed its importance.

Benjamin shot to his feet, rushing to the exit gate window. The limo's driver rolled down the window, revealing a well-dressed woman. Rain dripped from her flat-topped black hat and rugged leather coat.

"Wransatra is it?"
she asked, her deep voice cutting through the storm.

Benjamin nodded, his posture stiffening.

"Mr. Colthorn and his family are the last to leave tonight. The community will remain closed for the rest of the week and into the next. A cleaning crew from the Helping Hand Cleaning Company is scheduled to arrive later. Make sure they're on the approved list and let them in, if they have not already made it through. Mr. Colthorn has requested you personally oversee this station. You are not to leave until you are relieved by another guard at 6 a.m. tomorrow. Any deviation will result in your termination. Do you understand?"

Benjamin's chest swelled with a mix of pride and nerves.
"Understood, ma'am!"

The limo moved forward as Benjamin opened the gate. Once it disappeared into the darkness, he closed the gate, sinking back into the office chair.

"{You got this, Benny. From here, it's only up!}"

But his confidence evaporated when the alarm buzzed again. A black SUV idled at the entrance gate. Its windows fogged. Benny squinted at the driver, a towering figure staring intently into his rearview mirror. Recognizing the short clean cut blonde hair and emerald eyes.

Benny hesitated before he rushed outside to meet them.
"Hey, Lincoln! You startled the heck out of me!"

Lincoln rolled down the window, his jaw tight as his fingers drummed impatiently on the steering wheel. His glare snapped to Benny, and the younger man's expression faltered into unease.

Anthony leaned forward, his grin softening the tension,
"You doing okay out here, Benny? You know how grumpy Lincoln gets when he's stuck in a storm."

Benny chuckled nervously, glancing between Anthony and Lincoln,
"Oh, uh, yeah! I'm fine. The rain's a bit of a pain, but it beats last week's power outage. Thanks for asking Anthony."

Anthony smirked and gestured toward the gate switch,
"Think you can open that up for us before Lincoln starts growling at everyone? It's been a long drive."

Benny's eyes widened as he reached for the gate controls,
"Oh, yeah! Sorry about that! Here you go."

As the gate creaked open, Anthony nodded approvingly,
"Good to hear kid. Just keep your head up, storms pass quicker than they feel."

Benny chuckled again, a little less nervous this time,
"Thanks Anthony. Stay safe out there okay?"

Lincoln leaned back, gripping the steering wheel tightly,
"Keep those service windows locked Benny. It's going to get worse tonight, and the last thing we need is another flooded station. Got it?"

"Yes sir!"
Benny replied sheepishly. Heading back into the station, he locked the windows as the SUV rolled forward leaving the light of the flood lights.
"{This is going to be a long night.}"

Time dragged as rain and hail battered the shack. Benny spun idly in his chair, his gaze drifting from the monitors to the purple-covered book.

"{Might as well read while I can.}"

Opening the book to the bookmark made by his id, he began to read. The text was dense, filled with tales of magic, war, and divine curses. His lips moved silently as he mouthed the words, his brow furrowing at the descriptions of bloodshed and betrayal.

Putting down the book, Benny called out to no one, acting as if he were being answered. "Holy moly, what kind of book is this, June? I'll definitely have to save this for later. Magic, monsters, gods, and devils. I love reading fantasy!"

Thud ... thud, click-click-click.

Benny glanced at the control board, cycling through the multitude of cameras. Each one buzzed to life, though many of the outdoor feeds were obscured by water droplets and fog. A few cameras in the Rec House and Maintenance Garage weren't responding at all.

"{Maybe the storm is causing some glitches. Better report this in.}"
Pulling up the feed from the western shack, he spotted Drake striking a filing cabinet. Papers and a chair were scattered across the floor.

"{Maybe I shouldn't bother him right now.}"

The thought of Lincoln yelling at him for not reporting it in made his stomach churn.

"{AAAGGGGHHHHH!}"

Clicking his bracelet nervously, he made a call.
"[Drake?]"

Drake's back faced the camera as he pulled his hand free from the hole he had punched through in the filing cabinet.

Benny sat still, his shoulders tense.
"[Hey, Drake? It's me, Benny.]"

Drake raised his bracelet to his face, tapping it twice before replying in a voice as cold as ice.
"[What do you want?!]"

Shuddering in his seat, Benny stammered, "[A few cameras in the Rec House aren't responding. Want me to call Lincoln to check them out for you?]"

"[No!]"
Drake snapped back.

Benny froze, unsure of how to respond. After a beat, Drake's tone softened slightly.
"[My brother taught me some things about electronics. Don't worry, I'll handle it.]"

"[You sure? I don't want to force you to go out in this storm since you don't have a ride.]"

"[It's fine Benny. I could use the air.]"

"[Alright.... I'll call you once they start responding again.]"

Both clicked their bracelets, ending the call.

"{Dummy, dummy, dummy... Lincoln strictly told me not to let him leave his station. *But Mr. Colthorn said I'm in charge.* Crap, what do I do?}"

Benny considered lying to Lincoln but quickly dismissed the idea, imagining all the different ways it could go wrong.

"{AAAAAAAGGGGHHHHH!}"

Shaking nervously, he clicked his bracelet again. "[Hey, Lincoln, it's Benny calling in.]"

Lincoln's proud voice came through the bracelet. "[I hear you Golden Tower. Knight One here!]"

Benny gritted his teeth, forcing himself to sound calm.
"[I wanted to report some cameras in the Maintenance Garage that are not responding.]"

"[Got it Golden Tower. Write up an incident report and keep monitoring. Let me know when they're back online. I'll check in if anything comes up.]"

"[Roger that!]"

"[Anything else? How's our new friend holding up?]"
Lincoln stated in a cold belittling tone.

"[Uh... yeah. Everything's fine on his end.]"

"[Okay Golden Tower. I'll do a surprise checkup when I'm done here. Keep an eye on his camera and let me know if he leaves or if his brother shows up. Knight One out.]"

"{Dang it! Dang it! Dang it! I'm going to be in so much trouble! I lied to Lincoln, and it's probably just a dumb bug with the cameras.}"

His gut voice snarked,
"{*Technically, we didn't lie. Besides, Lincoln's too simple to figure it out.*}"

Benny shot back,
"{He's not simple! He was a surgeon and field doctor during the Great Northern War!}"

The voice mocked him,
"{*Oh, sure. And now he rides us for no reason. And why do we have to write the incident report?*}"

"{He just wants me to do an excellent job! He said I'm the best at writing reports because I'm so detailed.}"

"{*Lazy. That's all he is. He doesn't want to do the work himself.*}"

Benny stood abruptly, a pain rushing across his mind, shouting as if defending Lincoln in an argument against himself.
"{No! He's the boss. He has so much on his plate. I want to help him however I can!}"

A struggle overtook Benny's mind, the hateful voice clawing at his thoughts. Grabbing his head, his vision blurred for a moment before snapping back. His gaze was drawn to a figure just outside the reach of the floodlights. Benny froze, his heart thudding loudly in his chest.

The storm seemed to pause; the howling wind replaced by the faint scrape of something shifting on wet asphalt.

"Wait, what is that?" Benny whispered, his voice barely audible over the rain and the static hum of the monitors.

Leaning closer to the window, he squinted at the figure. As a streak of lightning illuminated the scene for a brief moment, revealing a tall, angular silhouette. As the light of the lightning flickered, the figure shifted slightly, its head tilting as though it were looking directly at him.

Benny's fingers hovered over the radio controls. "{Do I call it in?}"

"{I wouldn't you're the boss you can deal with it.}"

Chapter 5
Ethan

Drip... Drip... Drip...

Felicity walked under the clubhouse patio from the downpouring storm, shaking off her umbrella.

"Damn rain. If the storm wasn't bad enough... *sigh!*"

Felicity's mind replays the scene,
"Drake was about to eat Lincoln. Heheheh..."

She blushes as a sickening smile formed on her face, but she shook it off before entering the clubhouse.

Stepping inside, she calls out for Baillie & Ethan, her voice echoing across the walls.

"Where are those two idiots?!"

"HELLO?!"

Her face turns a bright red, and the ends of her hair begin to stand up. She stomps in a circle on the hard granite-tiled floor.

"OH, COME ON! ARE THE TWO OF YOU NOT DONE CLEANING YET?!"

"HELLO!! FINE THEN! WHEN I FIND YOU, I'M HITTING ETHAN, YOU LITTLE WHELP!!"

Walking through the lobby, she holds her umbrella tight to her side, passing long towering walls covered in salt-brown wallpaper. The iron lamps around her reveal colorful oil paintings greeting her as she stomped to a wondrous staircase at the end of the lobby. Scaling up the stairs, her hand glided across the smooth beautiful red varnish.

...Wush...

The sound of wind rushed behind her through the open halls near the main doors.

...CRASH...

A vase shatters onto the ground at the end of the hallway to her left.

Spinning her head to see the shattered pieces, her rage quickly dissipates.

Still gripping the cherrywood handrail, the lights around her begin to shut off one by one until the ones above her go dark.

Another rush of wind calls out from behind her. Turning toward the hallways leading to the main doors, she peers into the darkness. But in the thickness of the shadows, she can only make out the shape of a bald figure with long horns protruding from its head. A faint, acrid scent wafts toward her, burning her nose. Suddenly, the image of a dark flaming soul becomes visible to her. The heat radiates from the figure, almost unbearable, but it captivates her in a way she can't describe. She stares, awe-struck, trying to speak, but before she can get any words out, the figure turns and leaves slamming the door behind itself.

Just then, a light turned on down the hallway to her left. The shattered pieces of the vase gone.

"What the heck is going on here?!"

Slowly, she makes her way toward the light, fighting each step until finally reaching the end of the hall. The light quickly shut off, and the sound of footsteps rushed all around her.

"RAWR!!!"
"rawr!"

WHACK!

"OW!"

Ethan and Baillie, dressed in devil masks, jump out from both ends of the open hallway, attempting to scare Felicity. However, it only reignited her rage and left Ethan with a rather large lump on his head.

The lights turn back on as Ethan rubs his newly acquired welt.

"Wha—wha-what the h..."

But he is quickly silenced with another whack from the umbrella in Felicity's hand.

"OW!!"

"What—me?! WHY! You little whelp!"

Baillie stood behind Felicity, laughing uncontrollably.

"AND YOU BB!!"

Felicity stops, turning to point her umbrella at Baillie, but it is missing. Spinning back toward Ethan, she finds he's already gone.

"What th..."
Pg.39

"I'd love to stay-stay-stay... and cha-cha-chat, but
I've got to meet- meet-up with Drake!"
Crying out as he rides the handrailing down the
staircase.

"LITTLE WHEL-"
Felicity tries to catch up to him, but before she
reaches the stairs, the main door slams behind
Ethan.
Baillie meanwhile, continued laughing, now rolling
on the floor in hysterics.

His run turns to a slow walk as he leaves the beast to
melt from her anger. Flicking the button to his new
umbrella.
Click

"{Jeez, just as angry as Mom and as strong as your
dad. Yeah, she is definitely your type, big bro.}"

The storm intensifies outside, hail mixing with the
rain, and bolts of lightning illuminating the sky.

"Ma-ma-ma- man, it's coming... Coming down
tonight."

Ethan's thoughts swirl, forced to the surface.
"{If the park was going to be empty for a whole
week, why didn't we do this any other day? Doesn't
matter, huh? Yeah, if she says jump, you don't ask
you just jump. It's like he forgot! ...Of course he did!
He left me behind!}"

Twisting with sudden anger, Ethan shouts into the
storm as a pain rushes across his head.

"WE.. WE.. WE WERE SA-SA-SUPPOSED TO
FIND MY DAD TO-TO... TOGETHER!!"

Pg.40

Grabbing his mouth,
"{And this stupid stutter... he said he'd help with
that too!}"

Images of the past were forced through his mind,
but he pushed them away trying to calm himself.
The pain in his head quickly leaves.

"{I've got to live for the two of us huh?}"

Sigh

"{Man, how far away is this place?! You'd think he'd
would have told me how far it is. Would have been
better to bring my scooter.}"

Reaching the front of the western guard station.
Anger still churning in his mind.

Looking through the windows of the guard shack,
he noticed the filing cabinet knocked over and
documents littering the ground. The only door is
locked, indicated by the red light on the keypad.

"{What the heck man? You were supposed to meet
me here. Looks like I'm not the only one messing
around. Hopefully one of the other guards isn't
with him... or worse, he got into another fight.}"

Thinking, Ethan pulled up his caster net bracelet. Tapping it twice, a small blue holographic screen appeared. Swiping across the screen, he switched to a map of the park. Seven blinking red dots mark the locations of: Lincoln in the northern part of the park, Anthony leaving the eastern guard station, Benny in the southern guard station, Felicity and Baillie at the main clubhouse, Ethan at the western guard station, and Drake heading toward the Rec House.

"{Well, he's alone at least. But it looks like he started without me.}"

Rubbing his face, Ethan headed toward Drake's marked location, staying far from the shack's cameras. Double-clicking Drake's red dot and holding his bracelet, Ethan tried to call him. The bracelet rang but no one answered.

"[Hey, dimwit! You- You were sa-sa-supposed to wait... Wait for me!]"

Ethan called again. But there was still no answer. "[Fa-fa-fine! I'll me- meet you there! Just... just don't touch. Touch. Touch Anything!]"

Pouring anger twists his mind once more. Gripping his head briefly, a sharp pain rushed in and out. Stomping through puddles and dodging hail, he marched to the Rec House.

Entering the western residential area, the lavish mansions stood empty and cold. Their lights were off, and their windows covered by heavy, colorful drapes. Each home mirrored the others, like products pressed from a factory line. As if they were built for function, not soul.

The streetlights guided Ethan's path, their faint glow the only thing keeping the inky darkness at bay. The night seemed alive, shadows creeping and curling around every corner, like predators waiting to pounce. He'd lived his whole life surrounded by the darkness of thieves and criminals, but this—this felt different. The sterile, orderly streets felt foreign, like the houses themselves were silently judging him, wishing him gone. A chill ran down his spine, not from the storm, but from the oppressive sense that something was watching him.

The wind howled, ripping the umbrella from his grasp despite his desperate hold. Lightning split the sky above, striking the grand clubhouse with a deafening crack. A pulse of white and blue light flared, for a moment the streetlights surged brightly—before popping one by one. Darkness closed in, suffocating in total.

Ethan froze, blinking through the rain, when he saw it. Two crimson eyes glowing faintly in the distance. They stared, unblinking, like they had seized his heart ready to crush it. Rubbing at his rain-soaked eyes, he hoped he was imagining things. But the eyes were still there, and they had moved closer. His trembling hand raised his c-net bracelet, activating the flashlight.

The glow revealed a nightmare.

Before him stood an emaciated beast, patchy raven-black fur clung in uneven clumps to its skeletal frame. Its sunken eyes glowed with an unnatural crimson hue, set deep within a grotesque, misshapen canine skull. The creature had no ears, and its jaw was lined with jagged, uneven teeth, jutting out at impossible angles like shards of broken glass. It growled, low and guttural, lifting its head to sniff the air before snapping its gaze back to Ethan. For a brief moment, it looked past Ethan into the darkness, as if something else had caught its attention. Then its crimson eyes locked back onto him.

Ethan stumbled backward; hands outstretched.

"Wo-woah there, da-da-doggy,"
His voice trembling as much as his body.

The beasts growl deepened, its body lowering as it prepared to pounce. Without warning, it launched itself at him. Ethan barely dodged, twisting to the right as he stumbled into the rain-soaked grass. The creature skidded but quickly regained its footing, spinning back toward him. Its claws glinted in the flashes of lightning, the sound of its growl vibrating deep in Ethan's chest.

"{WHAT THE HELL IS THAT THING?!}"
Ethan's mind screamed as he broke into a sprint, his boots splashing through the muddy lawns.

The beast gave chase, its claws scraping against the pavement with an ear-piercing screech. It leapt, clearing twenty feet with terrifying ease, landing mere inches behind him. Ethan spun, narrowly dodging another swipe. For a moment, he thought he had escaped unscathed, but then a searing pain tore through his right hip. His jumpsuit and skin had been cut clean, warm blood had begun trickling down his leg, mixing with the rainwater pooling in his boot.

The predator and prey locked eyes again. The beast crouched low, its powerful legs coiled like springs, ready to strike. Ethan's fear held him frozen, but his mind raced.
"{It's studying me, just like I'm studying it. But I can feel it—it wants me as its food.}"

Lightning flashed across the sky, momentarily blinding both of them. In that instant, Ethan noticed the creature's eyes struggled to refocus after each lightning strike.

"{That's my chance!}"

Timing the next flash, Ethan feigned left, then launched himself backward. Using the momentum, he jumped up the side of a nearby mansion. His soaked hands scrambled against the slippery shingles, but he managed to pull himself up.

The beast followed, leaping impossibly high and landing on the roof with ease. Ethan ran across the incline, the wind threatening to throw him off balance.

"{You like jumping, huh? Let's see how you are at falling!}"

Climbing even higher up the mansion, the beast inches from his heels. Ahead, he spotted his target: a greenhouse about eighty feet below. Sliding into the right spot the beast lunged, teeth bared, but Ethan dove at the last second, rolling away as it missed. The creature twisted in mid-air, clawing at empty space before crashing through the glass and steel dome. The sickening thud of its landing was followed by an agonized cry that echoed through the storm.

"Boom! BA- baby! Suck on tha- tha- that!" Ethan's adrenaline-fueled victory dance was cut short as pain flared in his hip, dropping him to his knees.

Sliding off the roof's edge, he caught himself on a window ledge. Forcing it open, he climbed inside, collapsing onto the floor.

"{I've heard of exotic pets, but that thing was ridiculous. Where do you even get something like that?}"

Pulling himself up. His c-net bracelet's light illuminated the hole in the greenhouse below, the beast was gone. Ethan's stomach tightened as he raced down the stairs to investigate. Reaching the greenhouse, his worst fears were confirmed: no sign of the creature, just a pool of black slime where it had landed. The viscous liquid gave off a faint acrid smell, unlike anything he'd encountered before.

"{What the hell is this stuff?}" His blood mixing with the slime as it dripped from his wound.

"Crap!"

Clutching his side,
"{I need to find a first aid kit.}"

His search through the house was frantic, each step
sending sharp pains through his body. Finally, he
found a cabinet stocked with bandages and
painkillers.
Cleaning and wrapping his wound, he couldn't help
but pocket a few extra pills.
"{Whoever owns this place owes me anyway.}"

Stepping back into the storm, he hesitated,
gripping the door handle tightly. His rage bubbled
to the surface. "{Where are you, Drake? You said
you'd protect me!}"

His thoughts turned bitter.
"{Probably off thinking about Felicity.}"

Mimicking Drake's voice in his mind, "
{Went to blow off some steam little bro. Can't let it
affect the job.}"

"{Yeah right!}"
He slammed the door but froze when the faint
sound of a child crying cut through the storm.
Scanning the dark, rain-lashed street, he struggled
to see anything. His flashlight flickered, the cold
zapping its strength. The cries grew louder, getting
closer.

"BIG BROTHER! ... BIG BROTHER PLEASE HELP
ME!"
Ethan stopped in his tracks, his gut twisting.
"{I can't stop. No one's supposed to know I'm here
with Drake.}"
Yet the cries pierced him deeper than the beasts
claws.

Pg.47

"{*But I'm not here with him,*}"
his thoughts countered.

"{*He left me behind.*}"

The cries turned to screams, mingled with the beasts familiar growl. Ethan's resolve wavered as the storm raged around him.

"{I can't compromise the job. What could I even do?}"

Another voice answered from within,
"{*Don't Ethan, it's a trap.*}"

Gritting his teeth, Ethan turned and ran toward the sound.

"{I can't do anything to help!"}
But his legs carried him forward anyway.

Ethan moved not by his own will but by some deep, subconscious urge to save someone else. To be a hero wasn't something Ethan believed he was capable of. He could only be a coward. Yet, with his wounds screaming at him, he ran faster than he thought possible.

However something inside him shouted for him to stop; clashing with what he thought his instinct wanted of him. This new voice was weak and was drowned out by the first inner voice roaring louder, overriding his fear, until Ethan heard the guttural growl of the beast standing directly in his path.

The flickering strobe of his flashlight and sharp, fleeting flashes of lightning illuminated another creature. "{This one had to be different}"—its fur was patchy, streaked with unusual colors, and black spots dotted its left side. Rain slicked off its fur in jagged rivulets. Each time the beast opened its mouth a bright red flame leaked out, and its claws scraped deep grooves into the soaked concrete. The beasts eyes locked onto Ethan's, freezing him in place. His body grew numb, refusing to obey him.

"{How many of these things are there?!}" The beasts ears perked at the sound of a child's cry behind Ethan. Breaking its gaze, the creature lifted its head, growled, and leaped past him toward the sound. As if freed from chains, Ethan felt his strength return. The unknown ideals rushed through his head, and for one brief moment, he surrendered to the will.

"{Oh you've got to be kidding me! Aagh! Fine! But only because Kat would have wanted me to be better.}"

He turned, sprinting after the beast and the child's cries. By the time Ethan caught up, the beast had already pounced. But instead of screams of terror her laughter echoed unnaturally, hollow and discordant, sending shivers down Ethan's spine. There was an acrid smell lingering in the air, sharp and chemical, seeping from her as though she carried it with her.

"{Wait... is she laughing?}"

"Um... He- hello? Are... are you o- okay?" Ethan's voice shook as he called out.

The beast froze, slowly turning toward him, a low growl rumbling deep in its chest. Ethan raised his flashlight, its beam trembling in his unsteady grip. Lightning struck, illuminating the scene in a strobe-like flash.
The child, if he could even call her that, stood before him, her appearance burned into his mind.

Leathery red-purple skin glistened in the rain, marked by white tattoos of strange symbols spiraling up her arms and across her face. Her feline-like eyes glowed faintly from a misshapen skull. Two small sharp horns poked out from her head, partially obscured by long ash-blonde hair tied with delicate blue ribbons. She clapped her hands, giggling with delight. Her movements were too smooth, as if her joints didn't quite follow natural rules.

"{Is this... a five-year-old? What is she?}"

"Yay, I win! Daddy is going to be so proud of me! Cookie-cake?"

The beast stiffened; its body coiled.

"Wa- wait. Wh- what... COOKIECAKE?!"
Ethan stammered.

The child's expression darkened. She pointed at him with a tiny finger,
"DEVOUR!"

The beast lunged. Its glowing eyes locked onto Ethan as if marking him as prey. Her eyes ignited with a dark purple flame, her lips moving in an eerie chant. Ethan's body turned to stone. He couldn't move, couldn't scream, falling to his knees.

His heart slammed against his ribs; each beat a desperate scream for survival. His chest heaved, but no breath came. A suffocating warmth spread through him as though his body was being drained of life. This wasn't just fear; it was something else. His mind cleared suddenly; the compulsion that had driven him earlier faded & the searing pain of anger that flooded his mind left him. Something she had been doing was controlling him, twisting his cowardice into false heroism. And now, as her chant dropped away, so did that illusion.

He was fully himself again: helpless, broken, terrified.
The beasts roar drowned out all other sounds. Pouncing at Ethan it dived for his chest. Time slowed, the freezing rain and pain from his wound vanished, replaced by a heavenly warmth.

Images flashed through his mind, rewinding his life like a distorted film reel. They stopped on a single memory.

The sweltering summer heat warped the air above a cracked asphalt road lined with run-down houses. A younger Ethan. No older than the monstrous child before him. Sat on a rotting porch, tears streaking his bruised face. His shirt was torn, blood trickling from his nose as distant sirens faded into silence.

"Hey, you okay little man?"

Ethan didn't answer. Instead, he threw his arms around Drake, clinging to him like a lifeline.

Drake winced but managed a weak smile.
"Alright, let's clean up that nose, okay?"

Pg.51

Ethan nodded, flinching as the rag touched his face.

"Hold the ice with the rag. It'll hurt less,"
Drake smiled firmly.

Ethan did as he was told, sniffing through his tears.
"I-I-I- I-I I'm sor-sor-sorry"

"It's okay little man. She barely hurt me, but I want you to know that you can say whatever's on your mind. Even if it's hard. I'll listen,"

Ethan's lip quivered, and more tears spilled over. He dropped the ice and wrapped his arms around Drake again.

Drake hugged him back, his gaze shifting toward the horizon as if ensuring they were truly alone.

"Listen Ethan,"

"We've gotta stick together now. If we don't, we won't make it. You're the brains, you've got a lot going for you, and I'm not letting that die. I'll live for the two of us, okay?"

Chapter 6
Drake

Pat. Pat. Pat.

The drops of water smacked against the hard white tile floor of the western guard station. The air was stale, carrying the faint metallic tang of rust and cleaning chemicals. A flickering fluorescent light above casted a long wavering shadow across rows of filing cabinets. The faint hum of the station's backup generator blended with the relentless drum of the rain outside. Forgetting to close the door behind him, Drake's eyes glossed over, his face empty and expressionless. He staggered toward the first solid object he could see.

BBAAAAAMMMM!

Striking down, he smashed the middle of the cabinet door, his fist punching in a sizeable dent. He struck again and again, each blow echoing through the station. His face twisted with foaming anger, his thoughts racing to Felicity, then to Lincoln. Their words replayed in his mind like a broken record, each repetition fanning the flames of his rage. Suddenly, he heard a voice call out his name, distant and familiar. For a moment, he was no longer in the guard station. The freezing cold winds of that day surged through his mind, the deafening sounds of gunfire and desperate cries ringing out in all directions. It was too heavy to shake off. But then, the voice called out to him again, cutting through the chaos.

"[Hey, Drake? It's me, Benny.]"

Drake raised his bracelet to his face, tapping it twice before replying in a voice as cold as ice. "[What do you want?!]"

Benny stammered,
"[A few cameras in the Rec House aren't responding. Want me to call Lincoln to check them out for you?]"

"[No!]"
Drake snapped, Benny's words pushing the heist's importance back into his mind.

Sigh

Drake's tone softened slightly.
"[My brother taught me some things about electronics. Don't worry, I'll handle it.]"

"[You sure? I don't want to force you to go out in this storm since you don't have a ride.]"

"[It's fine Benny. I could use the air.]"

"[Alright.... I'll call you once they start responding again.]"

Drake clicked his bracelet ending the call.

Rain battered Drake as he stepped outside, the wind clawing at his clothes, forcing him to pull his jacket tighter. The storm was relentless, the rain coming down in icy sheets that blurred his vision. The occasional hailstones pelted his shoulders and head, the cold sting adding to his simmering anger.

Each step toward the Rec House felt heavier. His mind rebelled, dragging him back into the battlefield of his memories. Gunfire, screams, betrayal. They all clawed at his resolve. He clenched his fists and yelled into the storm; his voice drowned out by the roaring wind.

"AAHH!!"

BAAMM! ... CRACK!

Striking a nearby tree the bark splintered under his fist. Panting, his breath came in short bursts visible in the icy air.

Grinding his teeth, he muttered through clenched jaws.
"Out. Of The. Moment!"

Taking a deep breath, he pulled his fist back and spoke the words again quieter this time.
"I've got to stay out of the moment."

His mind fought him, trying to drag him back into the chaos, but he forced himself to stay grounded.

He slammed his fist into the tree one final time, his voice strained.
"Out of the moment, and where I need to be!"

Leaning heavily against the tree his knees buckled. Slowly, his breathing steadied.

Patting the tree's battered trunk,
"I'm sorry I took my anger out on you."

SIGH!

"{I'm trying, Doc}"

He tapped his bracelet, intending to leave Ethan a message about heading to the Rec House. But as he pushed the projected screen away, he didn't notice the message failed to send as the bracelet lost connection to the caster tower.

Continuing his march, he paused occasionally, scanning the storm-wracked landscape. A creeping sensation of being watched set in, gnawing at the edges of his awareness. The wind howled; lightning split the sky above as it struck the main clubhouse with a deafening crack. A pulse of white and blue light flared, and for a moment, the streetlights surged brightly—before popping one by one. Darkness closed in, suffocating in total.

The rain intensified, now mixed with hailstones the size of golf balls. He raised his arms to shield his face.
The Rec House loomed ahead, its silhouette stark against the storm's fury. The building was eerily dark, its exterior cameras lifeless, their indicator lights extinguished. Reaching the front door, he noticed it was unlocked. He propped it open with a nearby door stopper.

"{Did Ethan get here before me? Why did he leave all the lights off?}"

He flicked the light switch near the entrance, but nothing happened. Swiping his c-net band, he activated its flashlight mod. The beam revealed a chilling scene: bear traps scattered across the stairs and lobby, loaded firearms mounted on walls rigged to trigger wires.

"What the he—"

"That's just cheating!"
A young, squeaky voice rang out from the darkness, stopping Drake cold. He whipped his light toward the source of the voice, but nothing was there.

"I'm over here Fool!"

His light darted to the top of the stairs. A boy, no older than eighteen, leaned casually against the railing. His leathery hide was a deep, dark purple, almost black, and his two ram-like horns framed his immaculate haircut. His grin revealed sharp, glasslike teeth that shimmered faintly.

The boy's voice was eerily calm, carrying an air of cryptic mockery.
"Welcome Mr. Chambers. How do I know your name? That's not something you should worry about. You won't have time to ponder it anyway. What we have planned for you... well, let's just say it's far beyond your comprehension."

Drake's face hardened, his rage simmering just below the surface. He took a step toward the stairs, his focus locked on the devil. Smirking, the devil stuck two fingers into his own mouth, letting out an ear-piercing whistle. From the darkness behind Drake, growls echoed, low and menacing. Drake turned to see hulking shadows stepping into the light.

The beasts moved with unnatural fluidity, their eyes glowing faintly in the storm's sporadic flashes of lightning. They circled him, their wiry frames radiating a terrifying strength. One beast kicked the door stopper free, and the door slammed shut with a locking crash.

Drake gritted his teeth as his mind raced to what could have happened to Ethan. The beast on his right lunged first, claws swiping at Drakes arm. He caught its attack but felt the force push him back toward a bear trap. The beast on his left clamped its jaws around his ankle, its weight pinning him in place. Pain shot up his leg as the creature tore into his steel-toe boot, warm blood pooling inside.

"Already pinned down by a few mutts? Some Leviathan," the boy mocked, leaning against the railing as he watched.

Ignoring the pain, Drake grabbed the scruff of the beast biting his ankle. Using its weight as leverage, he heaved it backward into the nearby bear trap. The mechanism snapped shut with a brutal crunch. As the trap caught the first beast, the second lunged again. Drake twisted, planting his foot beneath it, snapped forward with a kick, breaking the creature's jaw. Panting, he forced himself upright, blood squishing out of his boot. His cold, quiet rage burned hotter. He wouldn't stop. Not until he knew Ethan was safe.

Relinquishing his smile, broken by shock, the young devil's face was quickly overtaken by gleeful mockery as he cheered and ranted,
"HA! *Your nothing like your cowardly brother*, are you? Running, hiding... *what a rat...*"

From cold to hot, Drake's face tightened, his jaw clenched as he held back a guttural growl that seemed to come from somewhere primal. Every muscle in his body screamed for release, but Drake refused to give in. His rage, a wildfire of grief and fury, clawed at his chest. "{*Focus, damn it. Focus on Ethan.}*"

"Where is Ethan?!"
His voice came out cold, rough, and sharp.

The boy spoke again, his tone just as mocking, eyes glowing with an amber light.
"Like I said... you don't need to know!"

He snapped his fingers, and the beasts surrounded him again, lunging just out from his sight. They looked as if they hadn't been harmed at all.

The first beast leaped for Drake's neck, but Drake managed to land a cracking left hook. Sending the beast flying into a nearby granite pillar.

The second beast changed course just slightly, sinking its teeth into his right shoulder. Standing at seven foot ten, it loomed over him, its weight forcing Drake back.
Yelling out in pain, Drake struck over and over at the beasts head, trying to force it to let go, but nothing worked. Each blow felt like his bones were breaking, but he couldn't stop. His body screamed, but the beasts growls fueled his fury.

Strike after strike, until the world narrowed to nothing but the sound of metal on metal.

As his hand reached out for another hit, he was stopped by a sickening crunch. Looking down, he saw the other beast biting into his hand, snapping his fingers. The pain exploded through his body. He pulled desperately at the beast gnawing on his hand, but it yanked harder, dragging his arm.

The warmth of blood rained down his chest, his vision fading.
"{*No. Not now. Not till I know Ethan is okay!}*"

The young monster clapped and cheered. His applause was a mocking sound of gunfire slamming into steel, driving Drake's vision elsewhere.

A snap of cold chills wrapped around him. Men and women screamed, some for medics, others crying in a language he couldn't understand. Bullets whipped past him, two finding their mark in his left shoulder and right arm. The pain forcing him to drop his rifle. Screaming, he grabbed his arm, more bullets zipping past. Then, a young blond-haired man tackled him to safety. Dragging him behind a small barricade.

The man's emerald-green eyes locked onto his with intense urgency.
"Get your mind out of the banks DC!"

The young man extended a hand to help Drake up. But as Drake looked, the joy in the man's face shifted to anger and shock. Now covered in blood, a clean hole had pierced through his skull. In a blur, Drake's heart fluttered, snapping under the weight of the memory.
Rage boiled over breaking the trance.

Letting out a monster-like roar, he bit into the beast latching his hand, ripping a sizeable chunk of meat from its neck. Yelping, the beast let go for just a moment, in that instant, Drake grabbed the beasts lower jaw, tossing it in the air. Catching the beast by its neck, he crushed it's windpipe; killing the creature. Spinning, Drake used the momentum to throw it across the lobby. Crashing through the glass walls that overlooked the garden hedge maze, it disappeared into the darkness. The second beast still clung to his shoulder, biting down even harder now, but Drake didn't feel any pain. Gritting his fangs, Drake shoulder checked the hound into a nearby granite pillar. Again and again, he slammed it into the stone. The rhythm of the blows was a trance in itself, a drum beat of survival. *One more, then one more after that...* His rage burned like a volcano, until the beast finally let go, its body crumpling beneath him.

"HAHAHA, now that's a show!"
The young devil clapped from the railing, his eyes glowing brighter with amusement.

"I bet you're still hungry for more, aren't you? You're way more of a show than your weakling brood. No matter—he'll be dead any minute now. Father will be pleased with me for bringing you back..."

Staring at the motionless creature in his hands, Drake's ears perked up. He turned to face the young devil, his voice a growl.

"That was it. Did that one finally hurt."

"WHERE! IS! ETHAN?!"

Pg.61

The devil laughed harder, his mocking tone ringing through the lobby.
"What does it matter to you? Wasn't it *you* who left him behind, running away? *Maybe you should've...*"

WACK!

Drake launched the crumpled wad of a beast, firing it like a bullet at the young devil. The beast flew through the air with such speed that it knocked the devil clean from the loft's railing. Leaping over sixteen feet, Drake cleared the loft's balcony and handrailing, landing effortlessly on the other side.

Rushing the devil while it was still pulling its self-up. Gripping the devil by his throat, he slammed it against the wall with such force that it left a sizeable dent in the stone.

The devil's eyes widened, the smirk faltering as he gasped for air.
"AACKEM!"

Spitting blood, the devil struggled, each attempt to move only met with another slam into the wall.

"TALK!"

His voice came out in ragged gasps.
"I. don't. know! My. sister was. to deal with him! He... is... already... dead!"

WHACK!

Drake slammed him against the wall again. The devil's smile cracked under the stress. Ears perking up again Drake heard the beast he had just put down sneak up behind him. Somehow the creature was seemingly undamaged again. Claws scraping across the floor before it could leap, Drake twisted, shoving the devil into the beasts open maw. Grabbing the hound by the belly, he hurled them both deep into the lobby.

"If you like watching beasts fight, why not join them and get front row seats?"

The two crashed to the floor, the hound immediately sinking its teeth into the devil's belly. Blood stained the floor, pooling around them.

Drake stood there, pulse pounding, fists clenched, eyes wild with desperation. His mind with only one thing on it.
"Where are you ETHAN?!"

Chapter 7
Ethan

Alone on the porch once again, now a young man, the world around him seemed to distort. The sun hung suspended, trapped in a permanent sunset. Ethan knew why he was here. Caught up in another person's hustle, "{AGAIN!}"

"{It's the same over and over again! Doing it all because someone I loved asked me to.}"

He looked down at his bloodstained hands. "{I at least tried. Didn't I?}"

His mind drifted back, replaying the kiss given to him. The tingles that lasted a moment longer, even after it ended. He also thought about that hug from Drake, the first time it had ever happened. He had never been hugged by his brother before, but that moment had been more than he'd ever thought possible. Growing up, he had always believed Drake hated him, that Drake blamed him for his father leaving them.

Looking back, Ethan wondered if he ever get a chance to see Kat one more time. He stared at the sunset, his gaze reflecting the disquiet in his heart. *"How could it have all come to this?"*

And then he heard it—the thundering of the beast barreling toward him, the hail and rain slamming against him. The little monster's laughter echoed in the storm. But another sound cut through, a shadowy figure sprinting toward him.
"{Oh great, another dog. Well, at least I won't bother someone in death by needing to be cleaned up.}"

But it wasn't another one of those creatures, it was Drake. Sprinting toward him, moving so fast that the water around him kicked up in waves. The beast, just inches away from Ethan, was struck with such force that it flew off into the distance as if it had hit an invisible wall shielding Ethan. Drake crashed to his knees beside Ethan, shaking him.

"ETHAN, WAKE UP!!"
He screamed, his tears swelling, but fading quickly as Ethan coughed up some rainwater. Hugging him, Ethan's tone was a mixture of relief and frustration.

"Ma-ma-man, you're slow. Wha-Wha-what took you so long?"

Drake pushed him back, quickly standing up. The sadness vanishing as annoyance replaced it.
"Well it's good to see that you're okay!"

Ethan shot up, panic consuming him.
"*WHER... WHER WHER WHERE IS SHE?!*"

Drake looked around, puzzled.
"Who are you talking about?"

Ethan frantically pointed behind him, but when Drake turned around, there was no one there.
"Wha wha what the heck?"

Pg.65

Drake shook his head, a sigh escaping his lips.
"Come on, quit messing with me."

Ethan's voice trembled, desperation in his eyes.
"There was a girl, a... de... devil girl!"

Drake patted his shoulder, trying to calm him.
"It's okay, I believe you. Take a deep breath and say it slowly."

Ethan inhaled deeply, trying to steady himself, and then exhaled slowly.
"When I... when I came to meet... meet up with you... you were... were gone. So I... started walking... then... I was attacked by a devil girl... and her beasts."

Drake rubbed his head thoughtfully, looking back toward the Rec House.
"Looks like you weren't the only one. I had two beasts to deal with as well. They don't go down easily. I have no idea what's up with the people here."

Ethan snapped his fingers suddenly, a side eye gaze taking over his face.
"May May Maybe contam... contaminated water?"

Drake chuckled, shaking his head.
"Maybe. But let's get out of this storm. We still need to get the money."

Frozen in shock, Ethan cried out, his voice laced with panic.
"NO! We... we need to leave! NOW!"

Drake lifted his hand from Ethan's shoulder, his expression softening, but determination still firm in his eyes.
"We can't Ethan."

"WHA... wha- wha- WHY?!"

Drake's face turned slightly red, frustration flaring.
"You know why."

Ethan's anger flared as well, matching his brothers.

Turning his head to the side.
"HUH?"

Drake locked eyes with him, his gaze hard. Drake opened his mouth, but before he could speak, Ethan cut him off with a yell.
"Oh... OH Yeah, THA-THA-THAT's Right! AND how WEL... Well-Well- WELL HAS OUR Sa... Sa... SAVINGS GONE, HUH-Huh-HUH, DRAKE?"

Drake sighed heavily, his voice lowering.
"We tried to save up for it, but things kept getting in the way."

"Oh... o- oh yeah, things! Funny how... HOW *things* are all- ALL- ALWAYS what you call it!"

Drake clenched his jaw, the tension thickening between them.
"It was many things, like bills, food, taxes, and your schooling!"

Ethan's eyes narrowed,
"Are ARE Are you sure tha- that's all the things Drake?"

Drake's face fell, and he turned away, the anger leaving his expression as he looked off into the distance.

"GO AHEAD, SAY... say- SAY IT! YOU NO- NO... KNOW WHY We- We- WE... DON'T HAVE ANY SAVINGS!!"

Drake stood there, motionless, his fists clenched. *"GAMBLING!!"*

Ethan's grin was cruel, *"YUM! IT FE- FE... SO- FEELS SO GOOD TO FINE... FINE- FINALLY HEAR IT!"*

Drake stood still, his body rigid with suppressed anger. He didn't move, he didn't speak, his gaze only looked down.

Ethan stared at Drake; his anger still hot in his chest & a pain now rushing across his head. But then something else, a flicker of the brother he had once known cut through. The memory of Drake's hug, that rare moment of warmth, haunted him. But no, the pain of betrayal was more familiar. *"{How could I still feel this way after everything?}"*

His mental wall went up again. Ethan took a step back, his voice breaking through the vulnerability. *"NO!"*

Drake reached out again, desperation in his eyes. "Please, Ethan. This is our last chance."

Ethan pushed his hand away, stepping backward, his eyes hard like stone. "Who- Who knows what they... Could! Have in there. Mon-mon-monster Dogs & Devil Children. It's like ah- ah- ah horror movie in there."

Pg.68

Drake reached out, trying to stop him, but Ethan moved further back.
"Please Ethan. You're the only one who can unlock the safe. I need your help to get the cash so we can finally leave this lousy island."

Drake's face broke from the hurt.
"I do want to help you find your Dad. I've always been looking, but I know I haven't done a good job at it, and I'm sorry Ethan. Please this time I need *you* to live for the two of us. Without you neither of us will be able to get the safe open and out alive."

Ethan clenched his fists, but his shoulders sagged slightly, betraying the weariness that came from carrying this pain for so long.

"*{I wanted to believe in you. I really did... but you left me with nothing but an empty house and memories of you telling me it would all be okay.}*"

Ethan stopped thinking, quieting his mind. His eyes looked into Drake's soul. A heavy silence hanging between the two, until Ethan broke under the memories.
"Fine. I'll do it. I act- act- actually *really need* the money too."

Drake placed a hand on Ethan's shoulder,
"Thank you Ethan. It will be just like—"

However, Ethan interrupts, his voice sharp, knocking away Drake's hand.
"No. I'll do-do-do the job with you, but... after this, we're done. You lef... Left me ALONE to- to- TO... to live and fend for myself in a CESS... cess-cesspool of a city."

Drake's face tightened, his frustration growing.
"There was nothing I could do Ethan."

Ethan tried to hold back the anger, but it broke free
for a moment.
"I WAS NINE DRAKE!"

Ethan exhales, frustration building in his chest.
"How was a nine-year-old boy supposed to pay bills
or buy food? With wha- WHAT job, with what
money? I ha... ha- had to stop going to school... and
do- do- DO the same work you taught me to do."

He paused for a moment, eyes full of hurt, before
continuing.
"I had to d- d... dro- drop out of those classes you
paid so much money for. Wha... what did you think
was going to happen if you got locked up?"

Drake looks sincere, his voice low with regret.
"I'm sorry Ethan. I had no other choice."

Ethan clenched his fists, the pain in his head
growing into a bonfire.
"Now- Now you say it... But not when you called me
for the ja-ja-job... OR when you had me meet your
girl... GIRL-friend. You lef lef LEFT me at the office
job & worse to live alone at nine for I don't know
how long..."

Tears rushed down Ethan's face,
You couldn't even write a dam la- la- letter. And
only NOW... are you saying sorry?!"

Drake's face fell, his gaze pained.
"I couldn't write to you. Not where I was."

Ethan's eyes narrow, sneering bitterly at Drake's words.
"An- an- AND why was that, huh? I kno- no... KNOW you can still write if you're in the army."

Taken by shock,
"How did...?"

"How did I know? Come on Drake, it's not hard to ha- ha- hack the district records in the pub-pub-Pub-... public library. I thought you were dead. They called you MIA, until, out of nowhere, I find out your alive and you'd been sent back years ago!"
Drake's eyes widen.
"So you know?"

Ethan stands a little straighter, the weight of his words sinking in.
"Yeah, I know you went into the army to lower your sent... sent... sent-encing. I know you were- were- were in the recent war. But what I don't know is why didn't you come home!"

Frustration leaves Ethan as he breathed out the words flooding his mind.
"Why couldn't you at least write to me? I wa- wa- was worried I'd never see you ah- ah- again. The police ta- took... took our house, and I had nothing Drake."

Drake's head fell, guilt heavy on his shoulders.
"I promise that where I was I couldn't write to you. But I'm still sorry Ethan. For not coming back to you or even writing to you when I was out."

Ethan scoffs, his voice still a bit shaky.
"Well- Well... Well, it's too late for being sorry!"

The two locked eyes, but Ethan quickly turned away, his face hardening.
"Let- Let- Let's just get this over with already. The soo... soo- sooner I can leave this hell, the better!"

But beneath the anger, there was a sadness that crept into his chest, the smallest trace of the bond that once was, still lingered. The silence between them stretched for what felt like an eternity. Drake didn't answer, his silence cutting deeper than words ever could. Ethan's jaw tightened, and he couldn't stop the next words from spilling out—words he'd held inside for years.
"I wanted you to be my brother, Drake. But you left me behind to survive on my own."

Drake's hand reached out again, but he hesitated, not sure if touching Ethan would make things better or worse. Ethan looked away, unwilling to meet his gaze.

"Please, Ethan..."

"This job... when we are done, let me help you. We can fix this if you give me a chance. We can start over."

But Ethan was already moving away, his voice quiet but firm. The words firing off like bullets
"No. I said-said- said we- we are done! Let's hur... hurry up and get this over with!"

Drake's hand lowered slowly, his expression falling, the weight of their broken bond hanging heavy in the air.

Together they walked toward the Rec House, but in their hearts they were alone.

Pg.72

Chapter 8
Drake

"Wha-wha-what do you mean you.. you... you don't have your keys?"
Ethan's frustration coloring his tone.

"I mean,"
Drake stammered,
"When I was fighting off those beasts, they must've knocked the keys off me."

"Crap. Hmm... There's gotta be-be-be a way to sneak in there."

"I could just smash the windows."
Drake suggested with a shrug.

"Nah- nah- no!"
Ethan snapped.

"Why not?"

"Because those devils... and their ma-ma-mutts. They'll hear us!"

Smugly smiling at Ethan,
"{Well you're not rusty that's good.}"

Drake scoffed, pulling his arms up and shaking his head.
"Yeah, you're right."

"If... if only there was a- a- another way in."

"Actually, there might be,"
A smirk creeped onto Drake's face.

"Yeah? How... how? I'm not climbing this bill-bill-building in the middle of a storm."

"You won't have to. I broke a window in the back of the lobby earlier—it faces the garden hedge maze. If you jump the hedge wall into the maze, you can sneak in and unlock the front door for me."

Ethan's face twisted in disbelief.
"You... You wa-wa-want me to jump into a heav... HEAV- heavily trapped bill-bill-building that prop-probably has those thing... THINGS waiting inside?"

"It should just be the little girl,"
Drake replied coldly.

"Wha-wha-what do you mean? Did you—"

"I did what needed to be done,"
Drake interrupted sharply, his eyes narrowing.

Ethan dropped his gaze, saying nothing.

"Come on,"

Drake smugly smiled.
"You said you wanted this done fast, right?"

Before Ethan could respond, Drake grabbed him, hurling him over the hedge wall.

"Don't scream!"
Drake whispered his yell.

"I—I'm injur...!"
Ethan's shout cut off by Drake's toss.

Drake sprinted back to the front door, pulling his c-net bracelet to his face. Tapping through the apps to locate the tracker, the screen flickering to static.

"Crap!"
He spat, looking at his signal bars to see a no connection indicator.

"{When did that happen!}"

BAM.

The sound jolted him. Looking up, he saw Ethan struggling to hold the door open, one hand pressed against his hip.

"What happened?"
Drake demanded as he rushed forward, pulling Ethan inside.

"U-u-you threw me too har- har- hard, you head-case!" Ethan barked, collapsing against the inner doors.

"Do you not know how to fall?"

"Before you sav... saved me, one of those beasts got me in the hip! I ban- ban- bandaged it, but you didn't give-give-give me time to tell you."

"{IDIOT!! How did I miss his injury! Get out of the moment Drake!}"

Drake's face tensed, regret instantly setting in. "I'm sorry. I didn't realize you were already hurt."

Ethan glanced at him, finally noticing the limp in Drake's step and the blood seeping through his torn sleeve.

"Your- your- you're hurt too,"
Ethan pointed at Drake's ankle and mangled hand.

Sigh.

"Yeah I got messed up too, but I'll do better at listening okay? Now let me take a look at your hip."

Ethan pouted, his cheeks puffing out as he grumbled, "It's a star-star-start."

Drake chuckled, yet the sight of Ethan's wound made him winced.
"Ouch little man. This looks pretty bad. I'm going to need something more than bandages to help you here. Did you see any of those things when you snuck in, or a first aid station?"

"No. Just some cartoonish traps & some- some pretty flowers."

"Can you walk?"

Ethan nodded with a grimace.
"I'll ne- ne- need something to dull... dull the pain."

He pulled out the bottle of painkillers he swiped from the mansion earlier. Popping two into his mouth,
"Aaahhh."

"Careful with those!"

Drake warned, shining his flashlight at the wound.
"They're not candy."

Ethan mimicked him with a mocking puppet motion, earning a glare.

"Hey, I'm just looking out for you!"

"Yea- Yea- yeah, you did such a great-great-great
job when you threw me,"
Ethan shot back, rolling his eyes.

"Hold still."

Reluctantly, Ethan let Drake peel back the soggy,
blood-soaked bandage.
"Let me see your first aid kit."

Pulling out a clean rag and fresh bandages,
"We'll need to stitch this up at a first aid station.
The kit doesn't have thread or needles. Or we could
always have Mack patch you up when we get
home."

Ethan smirked,
"If I'm getting stitched up, your-your-you're getting
worked on by Mack too."

"I'll be fine."
Drake's face holding back the fear of Mack with
needles.

"Ye-Ye-yeah, right. Look at your hand—you'll lose...
lose it if we don't wrap it up. How- how- how would
you even help yourself?"

Drake hesitated, side eyeing the comment.
"Fine! But stick close. Splitting up is a bad idea."

"Agreed."

Helping Ethan up, they moved cautiously into the death house. Stepping around traps, Drake broke the silence with his curiosity.
"So... how'd you get that wound?"

Ethan sheepishly looked away as he spoke.
"Oh, yea- yea- yeah, ha ha. I... I got one up on a roof, and thank-thank-thanks to the rain, I pushed it over. It... it had a really nasty fall."

Drake ruffled his hair with a grin.
"That's my brother. These brats think a few lousy mutts can take us down? They haven't met the Chambers brothers."

Blushing, Ethan smiled despite himself, knocking Drake's hand away.
"Sta- Stop it. If we keep following this path. We'll... We'll find the rec-rec-record room."

The two passed through the main lobby, the storm's roars muffled by the thick walls of the Rec House. As Ethan's flashlight swept across the room, he saw what Drake had described earlier. Traps lay scattered and triggered, some of the room's defenses neutralized, making their path easier. Yet, something gnawed at Ethan.

"There's no... no- no bodies,"

Ethan muttered.
"And none- none of that black slime."

Drake glanced around, his jaw tightening. "Looks like they were starving those poor things."

Ethan wrinkled his nose in disgust. "Gross dude. That's... that's not funny."

Drake's face darkened. He met Ethan's gaze, a rare moment of gravity settling between them.

"Hey, get a laugh when you can. Most of it's just scarring."

Ethan didn't respond, he just followed Drake to the service desk where a map of the building was posted. Drake studied it, then glanced at Ethan, who pointed at his c-net bracelet. Drake nodded, and the pair turned down a wide hallway.

The faint echo of footsteps—or was it just the creak of old wood?—kept Drake's nerves taut as they moved through the hall.

Ethan took the lead, carefully checking each corner. Drake noted the deliberate way Ethan moved—he wasn't about to let those devils get the drop on him again.

"{I've forgot how much Ethan prepares for these things. We should be done in no time flat.}"

The hallway's walls shimmered like polished gold, reflecting their flashlight beams. A row of narrow windows to their right revealed the storm's fury outside. Branches from the garden's trees whipped violently by the wind, scraped against the glass walls. Filling the corridor with an eerie symphony that it made the storm seem alive.

"Looks like even the trees wan-wan-want in," Ethan mumbled, as he pushed forward.

Drake had stopped, transfixed by the storm's ferocity. The way the shadows danced across the walls made it seem as if the storm had summoned an army to press against the rec house. The faint smell of damp wood and stone reached him, grounding him for a moment.

"Crap!"
Realizing he'd lost sight of Ethan.

"Ethan!"
he shouted, picking up his pace.

He followed the hall until it abruptly opened into a massive crimson ballroom. Chairs and tables had been pushed into storage along the edges, leaving the cavernous space eerily empty. The emptiness amplified every sound he made. Drake's footsteps echoing like intruders in a forgotten cathedral. Ivory and marble columns held up a domed ceiling adorned with strings of silver and gold, remnants of some recent party.

In the dome's center, a stained-glass window depicted three floating islands in a sea of clouds: one lush with plant life, one barren and desolate, and the highest bearing a shimmering city of gold and silver. The golden city seemed to glow faintly, its light almost alive, casting strange patterns across the floor.

"Drake!"
A whisper broke his reverie, pulling his attention to the right.

Spinning toward the sound, his flashlight beam swept the corridor, but Ethan was nowhere in sight.

"Come on, let's hur- hur- hurry up,"
the voice called, the cadence just enough like Ethan's to send a chill up Drake's spine.

"I... I think I found a first aid station o-o-over here."

Something was wrong. That wasn't Ethan, but Drake hadn't known that.

"Ethan?"
Drake called, his voice wavering. In the distance, he heard footsteps heading down another hallway.

"Ethan, slow down! Gosh, for someone with a bad hip, you sure move fast!"

He gave chase, following the sound of a slamming door. Drake skidded to a halt in front of four identical doors. No markers, no clues.
"Damn it, which one?"

Weighing his options, he chose the door directly ahead.

As he pulled it open, the unmistakable click of a rifle cocked. Before he could react, a shot rang out, striking his left shoulder. The bullet's impact sent a searing jolt down his arm, his fingers briefly going numb as the metallic tang of blood filled the air. The echo of the shot faded, leaving only his ragged breathing.

"Yep. Trapped. Of course,"
Drake growled through gritted teeth, his vision swimming as footsteps approached from beyond the corner.

He braced himself, muscles tensing.

"Alrighty you brat,"

"Come get me!"

The footsteps grew louder, coming closer. Drake lunged as a figure rounded the corner—and narrowly missed striking Ethan.

"HEY! Wha- WHA- WHAT THE HELL!"
Ethan shouted, his face pale as he stumbled back.

"You almost hit- hit- hit me!"

"But you?"
Drake demanded; his tone sharp.

"I went left! I turned... turned around, and- and- and you were gone. Then I heard a gunshot. What happened?"

Drake grabbed his head, groaning as if to clear the fog clouding his thoughts.
"I... I don't know. I thought I saw you go right."

"Jeez,"
Ethan exasperated.

"Don't-Don't-Don't make me get a leash. Come on... this is a dead end."

"But there was a door right there!"
Drake insisted, turning to point at the wall.

Ethan followed his gesture and shook his head.
"Right there, huh?"

Sigh

"I think the bla-bla-blood loss is really getting to you. Turns out, they- they- they moved the safe to some guy's office. I think his name's Tim- Tim- Timothy Cherrywood."

Drake froze, the name lighting a spark of recognition. Timothy Cherrywood—a prominent lawyer and surgeon from Lexington, known for his groundbreaking spinal and brain transplant surgery. Before his fame, Drake had known him as Commissioned Officer Cherrywood, the organ performer.

"Hello? Edrith to Drake!"
Ethan waved a hand in front of his face.

"We really need to get you some- some- something to eat."

Drake shook himself out of his reverie,
"I'll be fine."

Trailing behind Ethan, Drake grabbed the small loop at the top of Ethan's backpack, letting it guide him like a tether. Doubling back to the service desk in the main lobby. They entered through the intricately carved double doors behind the service desk. The pair navigated a series of hallways, winding past break rooms and small conference areas, until they reached an elegant door made of glass and oak.

Without hesitation, Ethan grabbed the handle—and immediately spasmed, his body jolting as an electric shock coursed through him. The door mechanism snapped shut, and a distant clatter echoed through the hall. Someone—or something—was coming.

"AAHHH!!"

"ETHAN!"
Drake's chest tightened as Ethan's scream tore through the hallway. His hands fumbled at the handle, desperate to stop the shocks.

He tried pulling Ethan's hand free, but the handle wouldn't budge. When Drake let go, the shocking resumed, drawing another cry from Ethan. The faint crackle of electricity echoed down the hall, like a taunt from the trap's designer.

Ethan, teeth gritted, fumbled into his back pocket and pulled out a small screwdriver.

"Pull... as hard as you can!"

"I am!"
Drake growled, his muscles straining.

"Pull harder!"

Drake yanked with all his might until the handle made a popping sound. Just then Ethan jammed the screwdriver into the mechanism.

"Pull me!"
Ethan commanded.

"What?"

"Just do it!"

Drake twisted around, grabbing Ethan's wrist and pulling with every ounce of strength in his body.

"Some- Some- some-thing has to give in!
E- e either the handle or my- my- my wrist."

POP-CRACKLE!

Drake staggered back as Ethan's wrist came free, leaving the door handle to snap shut, shattering the screwdriver in the process.

"Well, that was a close one,"
Ethan muttered, shaking his aching hand.

Drake glared at him.
"A close one? You almost fried yourself!"

Ethan ignored him as he whistled loudly.

"HEY!"

Drake hissed, clapping a hand over Ethan's mouth. Listening carefully, he realized whatever had been heading their way had stopped.

"If they don't know where we are, I'd like to keep it that way."

Ethan rolled his eyes.
"Stupid traps, that was my fav- fav- favorite screwdriver."

"This is what happens when kids have too much time and money on their hands,"
Drake grumbled.

"I wis- wis- wish I had that kind of money."
Ethan muttered, brushing himself off.

"Yeah, so do the other 99%."

The two surveyed the door. With no handle left to
pull, Drake decided to try pushing it.

"Let me handle this one,"
Patting Ethan on the head.

Drake tapped his right shoulder twice, steadied
himself, and threw his weight into the door. To his
surprise, it swung freely open, sending him
barreling into the office—and straight into a solid
oak desk.

CRASH!

"DRAKE!"

Ethan rushed in, only to find Drake sprawled across
the desk. He burst into laughter, doubling over
until he fell to the floor.
"Wow, smooth move big bear. You gonna knock
yourself out before they catch us?"

"You know, people usually ask if someone's okay
before they laugh!"
Drake snapped.

"Yeah, well, those people care,"
Ethan quipped, wiping tears from his eyes.

"Then why did you yell my name?"

Ethan didn't speak, instead just rolling his eyes.

Sweeping his flashlight across the room, revealing a simple oak desk, a computer, filing cabinets, an old oil painting of a purple stone dragon holding a tower made from the same stone; marked on its title was the Rainbow Dragon Kings Castle, and a corkboard with an inspirational poster of a cat dangling from a tree branch. The caption read:
Hang in there.

"Hey, yo, sweet find!"
Ethan declared

Drake raised an eyebrow,
"Seriously?"

"What?"

"It's- It's- It's a cool poster! If I die, at-at-at least I'll have this masterpiece,"
Ethan stuffed it into his backpack.

Drake sighed but said nothing, instead pushing several filing cabinets in front of the door as a make-shift barricade.

"See? I get my awe- awe- awesome cat poster, and you get to be the strong guy. Ev- ev- everybody wins,"
Ethan smiled smugly.

Drake studied Ethan carefully for a moment before speaking.
"Ethan, you okay? That zap earlier wasn't just nothing."
Ethan hesitated, avoiding Drake's gaze.
"I'm fine. Your- Your- You're the one acting weird, falling over fur-fur-furniture and seeing things."

"Yeah, maybe. But your hand is still shaking. Want me to check it?"
"No- no- no need. It's fine,"
Ethan turned to stare back at the empty cork board.
Pg.87

Drake frowned but didn't push further. He sat against the wall, watching as Ethan pulled out snacks from his bag. After a tense pause, Ethan finally sighed and tossed a couple of energy bars and drinks toward Drake.

"Here!"

Drake caught the food with a nod. Despite the silence, Drake couldn't help but think back to the last meal they'd shared—the night he was arrested.

They had just come home from an ATM crack. There were more vehicles on their street than usual, but Drake hadn't paid it any mind. To him, it seemed like another neighbor throwing a party—another event he couldn't care less about. They parked the van in the same spot as they always had, entering their home without a second thought. But that day would mark a mistake Drake couldn't forget.

Even though the man he'd killed had it coming for so many reasons, none of it mattered because the man was a Pearl Officer. Basically untouchable, there weren't many but for some reason this one had to get involved in Ethan's life. There was no time to breathe before their doors were kicked in and Drake was arrested. The protocol he had drilled into Ethan kept him safe from the raid. Drake had always known Ethan was a sweet kid; the streets hadn't hardened him yet. Ethan still thought of Drake as a hero. Both of them wished they could've stayed in that dream. But dreams end, and sooner or later, you have to wake up.

The present was quiet except for the crackling of plastic wrappers and the crunch of granola bars. From time to time, their eyes met, but whenever Drake tried to speak, Ethan would roll his eyes and look away. After a few failed attempts, Drake pushed through the discomfort.

"Is there any girl you like? Or someone you're dating?"

Ethan stared blankly at the oak desk. Words almost formed on his lips, but something stopped them. His expression hardened, leaving only a cold void on his face.

Drake brushed the back of his head awkwardly with his good hand

Sigh.

"Sorry. I guess it didn't end well, huh?"

Ethan's face didn't change.

Drake nudged Ethan's foot with his own. "Well, look at it this way—whoever it was, they missed out big time. You're one of the smartest and most acrobatic people I know. I mean, seriously, where did you even learn to do all that?"

For the first time, Ethan's features softened. A faint light seemed to flicker in his eyes.

Drake kicked at his foot again. "I'm serious. Remember that office heist when you jumped, what, twenty feet from a standstill? The last time I saw you, you could barely keep up with me!"

Ethan's lips twitched into a small smile.
"A group of friends taught me while you were gone."

"See? I knew you'd make friends out there."

"Yeah. They're the ones who helped me figure out where Dad is."

"Heck yeah. That's some great friends. Are they safe from the storm?"

"They don't have to worry. They're all dead."

Drake's voice hitched awkwardly.
"Oh. I... I'm sorry to hear that."

The silence between them stretched as Ethan crushed his energy drink can, tossing it aside.

"We- we we... can skip the small talk."

"Let- Let-Let Let's keep it like the office job. Remember? No small talk. Tha-tha- that was her rule."

Drake's head dipped; eyes fixed on the floor.

Ethan slung his backpack over his shoulder, standing back up.
"No idea how... the safe is sa-sa-supposed to be in this room. But we may a-a-as well look- look around."

Drake stood up heading over to the desk. Ethan watched him for a moment til he made his way over to the strange painting.

The drawers were disappointing—blank parchment, oil pens, nothing useful. But beneath the desk, scuff marks revealed it had been pushed recently. Leaning forward, Drake prepared to move it when Ethan tapped him on the shoulder.
"Look at this!"
Ethan whispered urgently.

Drake turned and saw the painting pushed forward, as though on hinges.
"What did you do?"

"I-I-I I didn't touch it!"
Ethan panicked.

"I-I-I was using my-my my black light on it, and I saw a mess- mess- message. Whe- when... I reached for the-the- the painting, it pushed in... like a door."

"Well, what's behind it?"

"I don't want to know. Wit-wit-with with everything going on, it could lead anywhere. Plus it's not on my map."

"What did the message say?"

Ethan glanced back at the hidden doorway.
"It-it-it it said the sa-sa-sa safe is in the hedge maze."

"Well, that's just a trap,"

"True, but-but-but it might also be r-r-r... our only way to get the safe."

"How? We're both in rough shape. Those dogs aren't gone, you know."

"This time we-we-we work together!"

"What's your plan?"

"Take... Take guns from the lobby. You handle the dogs, and I'll crack-crack-crack the safe with this.

Ethan pulled a bottle of squirming liquid from his backpack.
"I brought one of my favorite babies to make it quick—no-no-no one will see me. Plus if the safe isn't there, than we can make her tell us where it is."

Drake didn't like it. The thought of Ethan jumping into danger gnawed at him.
"What if the dogs get to you?"

Ethan pushed Drake's good shoulder.
"Where-where-where was this concern at the la-la last job? You lef-lef-lef left me behind when Felicity tol- told you to."

"And what a-a-a about after prison or the mil- mil-military? Did-did-did you ever come back for me then?"

Drake tried to speak but he caught himself.
"Shut up and listen!"

"You're the muscle. That's it. You-you-you-you don't get to worry about me. Not... after thirteen years. My plan works, and we'll get out. Then you can run-run-run off with Felicity, and I'll find my Dad!"

Drake reached for Ethan, but Ethan slapped his hand away.
"Let- let's just get out of this horror house!"

Ethan led the way, pausing to smack the handle on the door. When nothing happened, he opened it. Walking through he stopped for a moment in the hallway.

Sigh!

His face softened as he glanced back,
"Look, Drake, I'm sorr—"

However the door slammed shut, cutting him off.

"ETHAN!"
Drake shouted, slamming his shoulder into the door. He could hear barking and Ethan's frantic yells.

"I'm-I'm-I'm sorry all-all-alright! O-o-open the door Drake!"

The sounds grew louder until the door suddenly fell open. Drake stumbled forward, ready to fight— but there was no one there.

"What's wrong with you?"
Ethan asked, staring at him.

"You... you were yelling for me. The dogs were coming—"

"The door closed, and then you started beating on it," Ethan interrupted.

"Are you sure you're okay?"

Drake rubbed his temples; it felt like a fog rushed over his mind.
"I... I guess so."

"Come on. Don't let your shell shock of Cassady make this hard for me you big dummy head," Ethan muttered, slamming against Drake's mangled hand as he pushed past him.

Drake followed, lagging behind as they reentered the lobby in seconds. Drake's mind was blank, the fog fully consuming him as spirals overtook his eyes.

Chapter 9
Ethan

Beating on the door,
"I'M-I'M-I'M SORRY! O-O-OPEN THE DOOR
DRAKE!"

His mind raced as fast as the dogs barreled down
the hallway. Thoughts of Drake pushing the door
closed consumed him. Every word he'd said earlier
felt like a blade twisting in his chest, cutting deeper
with each passing second.

"Please, Drake! You still-still-still need me! You-
You-you said it... I'm the only one who can open the
safe!"

One of the Beasts finally turned the corner at the
end of the hallway. It's eyes locked onto Ethan as it
charged. Another two following behind it.

"..."

"DRAKE PLEASE! I'm sor-sor-sorry. I-I-I only said
those things be-be be-be-because I was mad!"
His fists pounded against the wood in desperation.

"YOU NEED ME! I-I-I-I THOUGHT YOU WERE-
WERE-WERE TRYING TO CARE!"

Through the snarls and ripping carpet, Drake's voice cut back, sharp and cold:
"I don't actually need you. I just need your backpack. You said it yourself. To open the safe, I need one of your special babies, not you. I'll let the dogs have a snack while I take the money and run off with Felicity. That's what you want right?"

"DRAKE NO! YOU-YOU CAN'T DO THIS TO ME! I-I-I I'M THE ONLY ONE WHO KNOW HOW-HOW IT WORKS!"

"Meh, if someone who can't even talk or spell right can work it. I'll figure it out."

The words hit Ethan harder than the pain in his hip. His legs faltered as the beast closed the distance.

"{It was always like this,}"

"{Everyone leaves eventually. Drake, Kat, even my Dad. But not this time. Drake's not getting the last word. I'll be the one leaving him behind!}"

The beast lunged; its glowing orange eyes pierced the darkness. Its black matted fur bristled, and acid-like drool hissed against the floor. Acting on instinct, Ethan twisted, reaching into his pocket he tossed a smoke bomb directly into its mouth.

The beast chomped down, smoke billowing from its mouth, filling its stomach and lungs. It fell to the ground, coughing and writhing in agony. The other two beasts, blinded by the growing haze, rushed toward Ethan but collided with each other, snarling and snapping in confusion.

Ethan sprinted, holding his side, he ignored the pain. Rushing down the multitude of hallways, he burst through the set of cherry oak double doors that led to the lobby. Ethan expected to dive behind the service desk. But instead, he tumbled forward, falling for only moments until he slammed into the hard white-and-gray granite tiles below.

Dazed, he looked around. This wasn't the lobby; it was the grand ballroom. He scanned the area in disbelief. The door he'd entered from had vanished, and there was no explanation for how he'd ended up here.

"(This... this doesn't make any sense.}" Clutching his head, the pieces wouldn't fit together in his mind. Someone or something was moving the layout of the Rec House.

"{But how?}" Tears welled up as he slammed a fist against the cold tiles.

"{Drake's just like everyone else—only out for himself! And Kat... she would've had a plan. She'd have kept us together. But then again... I'm the one that runs his big mouth, pissing people off.}"

Wiping his face roughly, Ethan stood. He couldn't dwell on it. The beasts already catching up, their barks echoed in the distance.

"{First, I've got to get rid of the dogs! I'll be home soon Dad.}"

He gritted his teeth and popped a few more painkillers, feeling their dulling effect stead his steps. Returning to the area where he'd split from Drake, Ethan opened a door to reveal a spiked pit with a rope dangling in the center. A grim smile crept across his face as his head filled with pain.

"Fine,"

"(You want me as bait? Let's see how you like it.)"

Pulling up his c-net bracelet, he loaded his smoke bombs tracker.
"{Looks like you swallowed the smoke bomb. Good!}"

He sneered,
"Time to turn these tables."

Ethan positioned himself by the door, eyes darting between the pit and the tracker.
"{Timing will be everything.}"

Waiting there he heard the beasts charging. Their claws cutting across the granite tile floor, like the sounds of knives being sharpened. Finally reaching him, the first beast lunged, muscles rippling as it closed the gap. At the last second, Ethan flung the door open. The beast yelped, claws scraping for purchase as it plummeted into the pit. Ethan slammed the door shut just as a sickening crunch echoed from below.

The remaining hounds hesitated. One whimpered, smoke still leaking from its mouth, while the other snarled and snapped at its companion, tearing at its horn.

"Are-are-are- Arguing now, are we? Figures. I bet-bet-bet you guys are as dumb as a rock," Ethan shook his head.

The two advanced cautiously. Ethan turned, only given a split second to sprint. He pushed all of his might into his still good hip and leg. Leaping over twenty-five feet, Ethan cleared the pit and grabbed the rope with both hands. The beasts skidded to a halt at the edge of the door, barking furiously.

Climbing higher, Ethan reached a small silver lever. Pulling it, opened a panel in the ceiling above him.

"Goodbye mutts!"
he taunted, pulling himself through the hatch.

Emerging on the second floor, Ethan found himself in an expansive library. The air smelled of aged paper & smoke. Looking around Ethan saw several trinkets adorned the mantle of a lit fireplace. A short sword, it's blade made from a matte teal-grey color. Awkwardly carved figurines of eight figures. Looking closer at them, there was one for each member of the park's midnight work staff. And sitting above was a painting of Lady Marrissa Myra.

Her smile glared down at him.

"Lady Myra,"
Ethan clenched his fists.

"{The great philanthropist. Except you stole from the schools you pretended to care about.}"

He remembered how her funding had been pulled just two years after he'd left school. The speech program that had helped him so much was dismantled, and Lady Myra's name was plastered on gaudy public buildings instead.

"Hypocrite,"
Ethan spat.

"{Eck! That sick smile, like she cares about anyone but herself. Once your husband died you dismantled the entire school. For what? An empty lot!}"
He considered ripping the painting down but stopped himself. Her smug grin would haunt him either way. Pushing the thought aside, Three beasts were still loose, but for now, he had a chance to catch his breath, he focused on his surroundings.

Scanning the room he found three doors out. Testing them, he found one to be fake, leading to a blank wall. The other two revealed vastly different hallways. One led to a dead-end streaked with blood; the other stretched long and open.

The sight of the bloodied hallway made his stomach churn.

"{That bloodstained hallway looks familiar,}"

Narrowing his eyes.
"{That must be the hallway where Drake had gotten shot in. They moved the rooms again!}"

He paused, listening carefully. The faintest hum of energy filled the space in the door frame. A dull purple glow vibrated across its surface.

"{They're not doing this randomly,}"

Pg.100

"{They're watching us. Cameras? Sensors? They have to know exactly when and where to shift the doors.}"

Pulling up his tracker again, he watched as his icon shifted across the map.
"{Maybe if I hack into their mainframe I can mess with the mechanics that they are using to move the rooms around.}"

Opening his bracelet's interface. Fingers trembling, he navigated through layers of encrypted files. Each second felt like an eternity, the possibility of alarms ringing in his ears, but something was odd. He could move through their files easier then he could on any other modem.

"{Hhhhmm, this little things got some juice, but not enough to go too deep. But I, ah,}"

"Heck Yeah!"
Finally, he broke through. Schematics of the Rec House flooded the screen, alongside notes on the traps.

"{Jeez. Talk about time and money,. No wonder Felicity wanted to raid their servers.}"

But yet there was no interface for the room relocation. Looking at the door frames again he couldn't find any mechanical gears or hydraulic bars. It was like the door frame was a portal to another door in the rec house.

"{That's impossible, teleportation technology? I heard the Key Company figured out how to mass produce particle fusion but... not worm holes. I thought it was only possible on paper, but this shows that it can be done. How?! ...and how many leagues is their tech past mine. I've got to see if I can find a place to go deeper. They have to have something about how they are doing all of this.}

But then he opened a file called The Moons Tears. "{What is this? A list of victims?}"

Ethan's stomach twisted. Names, dates, and grim fates filled the screen. It was a list of people that had been sacrificed for something called the *Devil's Harvest Ritual*. Council Members, District heads, philanthropist's, and other prominent figures were shown on video slaughtering each other during the day. Some even in the very library Ethan stood. Holding his mouth Ethan vomited all over the lavish rug that sat next to the fireplace.

"{How could you enjoy watching *that*?!}"

"(Actually never mind. I know a few that probably would get a kick out of that.)"

Still nauseated, Ethan dug further, noticing that all the cameras in the park were still broadcasting. Walking over to one in the corner of the library, it wasn't moving and didn't have its recording light on.

"{I thought the park was without power cause of the lightning strike? Why did the streetlights pop?}"

Looking back into the files, Ethan found that the main park wasn't normally powered. Instead there was a second subsection under the park where the main power was feeding to.

"{So wait. If the cameras are not powered by the main power and they are not recording. Then where and how is the broadcast going on?}"

Swiping away at his screen, he yelled out "COMMAND CODE: BADGER!"

The screen shook for a few moments til a small honey badger dug out from a hole in the projected screen. Moving across the interface, the small badger waddled over to the middle of the screen. Digging another hole it dug for just a few moments until it popped it's head back up. Double clicking the screen Ethan was led further into the database. Finding links to resident files, lab reports from Timothy Cherrywood, and a file called the *Purge Point*. Ethan had also been given a link by his badger to the stand-by camera access & another broadcast called the Moon Lit Blood Room. He tried to get access to both, but he needed a better inner-face. Forced to just choose the stand-by cameras.

"{To be honest, not seeing more political figures fighting to the death would probably be a good idea. I've seen enough of it on tv to begin with.}" Looking into the standby camera system he quickly found Drake & the other two beasts.

"{Drake's already in the hedge maze. And bonus... I've got one of those monsters sniffing the lobby. I better move fast or else I'll be left behind again.}"

Pressing back to the door without the blood-stained hallway, Ethan marched through. Busts of different figure heads line the wall next to him. Reaching the end of the hallway he came up to a smashed in wall. Ethan crept toward its railing, overlooking the main lobby.

"{Either I'm lucky or they want a fight. I like the latter but it's always what's below.}"
Looking into the main lobby, one of the beasts wheezed violently, smoke still spilling from its lungs. The other had charged through the lobbies broken glass wall heading towards the hedge maze.

His eyes scanned the remaining traps. The chandelier loomed ominously, its crystal knives glinting in the faint light of the lightning striking outside.
"{Time to make an Entrance. I'm not out just yet.}"

Ethan reached into his backpack, pulling out a small Bee-like robot. Placing it on his palm, he lifted his hand, giving it a platform to launch. The tiny machine buzzed to life, darting directly into one of the beasts eyes.
The beast froze, growling low as the bee landed. Its snarls morphed into agonized howls as the robot burrowed into its eye until it reached the beasts optical nerve. Stinging and biting down, it sent the beast into a wild thrash. With the beast momentarily incapacitated, Ethan seized his chance, pulling a small knife from his belt, hurling it at the rope holding the booby-trapped chandelier above.

SNAP! CRASH! Bang-Bang-Bang-Bang!

The rope severed cleanly, and the chandelier came crashing down on the beast. The falling chandelier triggered a chain reaction. Across the lobby, traps sprang to life—bullets riddled the walls, knives shot in all directions, and bear traps snapped shut with deafening clicks. Dust filled the air as Ethan dove behind the railing for cover.

Peering through the haze, Ethan saw the crushed remains of the beast beneath the chandelier's deadly weight.

"Man, it takes ah- ah- ah- a lot to put these things down,"
Brushing himself off.

"{If I'm lucky, I can sneak up on the other one while it's mauling Drake to death.}"

Sliding down the staircase's hand railing to avoid the bear traps at the base of the steps. Ethan landed lightly, making his way through the wreckage. Broken glass crunched under his feet. The beasts remains let off an acrid chemical smell. It's body had already begun to melt into black sludge. From the gunk, Ethan saw a set of guard keys.

Picking them up,
"AHA-HA,"

"{Dang thing ate his keys. Guess it needed the iron.}"

Watching the beast dissolve, Ethan pondered for a moment about the creatures.

"{What the hell even are these things! Some kind of video game monster? So when I saw it down in the greenhouse, it had perished from the fall. Well one thing can be said they definitely are not normal dogs. I feel bad for whatever had to be done to them to make them this way. I hope this is a mercy little monster.}"

He continued walking after pocketing the keys, approaching one of the mounted pistols on the wall. A few swift movements with his multi-tool disarmed the trap, and he pocketed the pistol, careful not to burn himself on the still-hot barrel.

"Four bullets left,"
Gripping the weapon tightly.

"{Gotta make it count.}"

His chest tightened as he thought of Kat. Her voice echoed in his mind, steady and unwavering:
"{Don't let it go to waste Ethan. You've got this.}"

With tears welling in his eyes, Ethan turned toward the broken glass wall, the storm raging outside. Rain and hail pelted him as he stepped into the hedge maze.

"{Maybe I really do let good things slip through my grip because I crush them when I should just hold them close,}"

The weight of his memories pressed down on him. "{You were always smarter than me Kat. Lend me some of your foresight one more time.}"

The storm lashed at Ethan's face as he crept through the maze, each step crunching on the hail-covered ground. Patches of ice glistened on the concrete path, forcing him to move slowly.

Every snap of a branch or rustle of the hedge walls made his heart pound. With his pistol raised, his finger trembled on the trigger, "{I've got to push through this.}"

"{I can't let Drake use me like a tool anymore. Not this time. This time I'll be using you to live for myself.}"

Turning a corner, Ethan's foot slipped on a patch of ice.

THUD!

His breath caught as he stopped inches short of a trip wire. His eyes traced the wire to a massive blade poised above ready to slice anything in its path.

"Da-da-da Damn it,"

"{Stay cool, you need to stay cool.}"

A voice called out from deeper within the maze. It was raspy and uneven, but unmistakable, it was Drake's.
"E-than, is that you?"

Ethan froze. His tracker said Drake was in the center of the maze.
"Plea-ase, E-than, HELP ME!"

It sounded like Drakes voice but it was broken, Ethan still hesitated.

"{That can't be him. It's has to be a trick.}"

The voice called again, closer this time. "E-than, plea-se! I've been loo-kin for you. I am very hurt."

Ethan gritted his teeth. "I-I-I-I I'm sorry, but no. You lef-lef left... me to die Drake. For-for- for all I care, this is your karma."

"Th-at was-n't me!"

Drake's voice pleaded. "The door lock-ed, and we got spi-lit up! Plea-se, E-than, trust me!"

Slowly walking to the next turn, he pulled out a pocket mirror from his backpack. Ethan crouched low and angled it around the corner. What he saw was truly fantasy. The voice wasn't coming from Drake. It wasn't even human. The last beast stood there; its jaw contorted grotesquely as it mimicked Drake's voice. Its glowing orange eyes locked onto Ethan's reflection in the mirror.

"E-than, are you still there?"

Ethan's hand trembled, almost dropping the mirror. But he quickly slipped it into his pocket.

Rushing back to the guillotine trap, he grabbed a coil of rope from his backpacks side. Tying one end to his ankle and securing the other to a hedge branch. He took out a small hammer slamming it against the concrete pathway, falling purposefully with a loud *thud.*

"AAHH!"

The crushing sound of hail grew louder as the beast approached.

"Are you hurt E-than?!"

Ethan grinned, his heart racing as he pulled out a knife.
"{Come on, mutt. Take the bait, you guys love a free meal.}"

The beast rounded the corner, drool foaming at its mouth as it stalked toward him, still rasping in Drake's voice.
"I am com-ing to save you!"

"PLEASE NO!"
Ethan feigned terror.

With a sickening smile, Ethan hurled his knife, striking the trip wire beneath the beast. The monster's glowing eyes widened in surprise as the blade above sliced down, cleaving it cleanly in half.

Orange blood pooled around its remains as Ethan approached.

"Hah! Four hearts,"
Kicking the creature's right half.

"{No wonder you outpaced me.}"

Ethan wiped his face, orange streaks mingling with the rain. Raising the pistol, he called out into the storm,
"DRAKE! COME OUT... COME OUT... WHEREVER YOU ARE!"

His head throbbed painfully, but he pressed on, his determination unshaken.
"{Why has my head been hurting so badly?}"

But he didn't stop to think. His body kept moving. It was as if someone was forcing him further. The hedge maze stretched before him, and somewhere within, the final showdown against his brother awaited.

Chapter 10
Dead Corp Sergeant DC

The chair creaked under the weight of Alex's body as his tongue dragged across its worn leather surface, leaving a slick trail behind.

"Give me the remote Davis, or I'll gut you from head to toe and make you into a new chair since the guards don't want to fix old Bettsy!"

Davis recoiled in horror; his face scrunched in disgust. "AAAGGHH! Alex, quit licking the chair! I've been waiting for this for over three weeks. You can wait your turn like everyone else does."

"Hush up now, you hear me!"
Alex snapped, his grin wild and unhinged.

"Bettsy likes it when I get naughty."

The leather was cracked, worn from years of sweat and neglect. Alex's tongue traced the grooves, savoring the tang of salt and old grease.

"'Bettsy tastes like history,'"
He purred, his grin splitting his face like a lunatic savoring forbidden fruit.

"Mmm, can't you taste it, Davis? The salt, the years of sweat and other mystery secretions? Bettsy's got flavor, my friend."

Davis shook his head, horrified.

"You're sick, man. I just want to watch Desperate House Husbands. We just found out that Tim heard his wife on the phone with her business partner about their affair when they took that business trip to the Four Season's Island."

Before Alex could reply, the loudspeaker blared through the facility:

"BBBBRRRRAAAAMMMM!

"RECESS TIME!

"ALL PRISONERS HEAD TO RECESS FIELD 1-A FOR RECREATIONAL TIME!"

"FOR ALL THOSE WHO DO NOT WISH TO PARTICIPATE, REPORT TO YOUR WATCHMEN FOR 24-HOUR SOLITARY CONFINEMENT!"

The announcement cut off with a sharp click, leaving an eerie silence in its wake.

Across the room, a man in a finely tailored jet-black suit with a purple tie slid a folder of paperwork across the table to Drake.

Drake, chained to his chair, glanced at the file with disinterest. Picking it up, he flipped through it quickly, his brow furrowing as he skimmed the pages.

The man smiled, a thin, sharp expression that barely reached his eyes.

"As you can see, we have all we need to put your brother in the system and extend your sentence by another fifty-five years. Child endangerment, contributing to the delinquency of a minor, failure to supervise a child, and a whole list of other offenses."

Drake's muscles tensed as the man's grin widened.

"And I mean a *lot* more. Enough to rope your brother in, too. But we wouldn't want that now, would we, Mr. Chambers?"

Drake sat motionless; his piercing gaze locked on the man. His voice, when it came, was low and dangerous. "Why are you coming to me about this?"

The man tugged at his tie nervously, coughing. "Well, you see, you're lucky, Mr. Chambers. The government would like to give you—and citizens like you—a chance to better your lives. Most men in your position don't get this kind of offer. But your name was drawn from a very selective pool."

"Drawn?"
Drake asked flatly.

The man gulped, loosening his tie further. "Yes, uh, random selection, you see. And here's the opportunity: instead of serving your time in prison, you can serve your country. We're offering you a chance to join a specialized military division. In exchange, we'll reduce your sentence dramatically and erase your brother's record entirely."

Drake's lips curled into a humorless smirk.
"Serve the country, huh? What's the catch?"

"No catch other than patriotism,"
Dabbing his forehead with his tie.

The man extended his hand toward Drake, who
didn't move. Instead, Drake's thoughts turned to
Ethan. His expression softened briefly before
hardening again.

"If you're being honest then I'll sign,"
Without warning, Drake lunged forward, his chains
rattling loudly. The suited man yelped, leaping
back and raising his chair like a shield.

"Ha ha, two for flinching,"
Drake gave a wicked grin.

"Relax. There's not much a chained man can do."

Still wary, the man slid the signing sheet across the
table.
"You have my promise. Ethan's record will be
destroyed, and you'll both be free once your service
is complete."

The suited man whistled for a guard, who brought
over a trash can. Lighting the files on fire, ashes fell
into the metal bin. Drake felt a lump of guilt. He
wasn't sure if he was saving his brother or dooming
them both. Drake's fingers hovered over the pen,
his mind racing. If he signed, he'd be giving up his
freedom in another way—a pawn in their twisted
game. But Ethan... Ethan could finally be free.

"{That was worth any price, wasn't it?}"

Drake stared at the flames for a long moment before signing his name away. "Guess the word is 'Hu-Rah.'"

Days later, Drake found himself blindfolded, transported to a high-security military base. When the blindfold came off, he stood in the stark fluorescent lighting of a sterile facility. Around him were rows of prisoners—250 in total—all selected under a new government bill allowing prisoners to serve in military roles as a form of rehabilitation.

But what the government hadn't told the public was that these prisoners were being subjected to grueling experiments & horrific body augmentation. While the News claimed the bases housing these prisoners had been all wiped out by an attack from terrorists, the truth was far darker. These bases were purposely bombed by their own soldiers to claim the deaths of all prisoners so they could wipe them from the record & use them as they saw fit.

The prisoners chosen for this program were classified under the codename Dead Corp. Officially, they were erased from existence, their identities wiped clean. They weren't soldiers. They weren't people. They were ghosts—nameless and faceless tools of war.

Drake was one of only five survivors from the original 38 who underwent the leviathan program's brutal body & strength enhancements. These experiments were designed to create super-soldiers capable of withstanding unimaginable punishment. Drake's body was pushed to its limits with increased muscle mass, testosterone supplements, and invasive surgeries. Wincing as a thick needle plunged into his arm, injecting a burning cocktail of chemicals. The pain coursed through his body, leaving him trembling with unnatural strength.

As part of the Thrasher Division, Drake's role was to support his team through chaos and destruction. Each team consisted of six members:

Cassady: The young, charismatic leader with long blonde hair and piercing emerald eyes. A man of kindness and respect, Cassady was the anchor of the group, inspiring loyalty and camaraderie even in the worst conditions. "You're not just muscle, DC," slapping a hand on Drake's butt. "You're the spine that holds this team together."

June & Rose: Identical twins in their teens and assault troopers, fiery and relentless. Their crimson hair & small frames belied their ferocity in combat. The two were inseparable, bonded by a shared history of surviving Lexington's brutal gang wars. "Stay sharp June," Rose muttered. "I don't need to save your ass again." June smirked. "Pretty sure it's the other way around."

Timothy Cherrywood: The team's medical officer. Arrogant and unnerving, Timothy's background as a privileged rich kid contrasted sharply with his twisted demeanor. Drake had always felt uneasy around him, suspecting a darker side to his past. "{Timothy's laugh was too loud, too sharp—like he enjoyed the pain a little too much.}"

Hugh: The defense and explosives specialist. Short and squirrelly, Hugh's nervous energy often led him to flee at the first sign of trouble, but his skills with explosives were unmatched. "You sure you're up for this?" Drake asked as Hugh fumbled with a detonator. Hugh scowled, "Sure as this!" *BOOM!!*

Despite the horrors of their missions, Cassady always brought the team together. He treated Drake with respect, pulling him back from the brink countless times. Snow and hail battered Drake's face as he trudged through the storm. The icy ground threatened to betray him with every step.

"Get your mind out of the banks DC,"
Cassady extended a hand to help Drake up.

"You're not just here to survive, DC. You're here cause we need you."

It was a weight he didn't ask for but couldn't refuse. Cassady's words felt like his own just years ago.

"Come on,"
Cassady urged.

"June and Rose have cleared the governor's building and Hugh's is already radioing the ransom. All we need to do is hold the LZ until Timothy gets here with the dispatch."

Drake nodded, shaking the snow from his shoulders. He glanced at the rifle in his hands, its weight grounding him.
"{Let's get this over with already.}"

As the snow whipped around him, Drake's mind wandered back to the interrogation room like always. The man in the suit had smiled so easily, promising freedom. Standing in the cold with a rifle in hand, Drake had wondered if the twelve years were up yet.

Just then, a small hand grenade landed next to them. The two couldn't react fast enough to throw it back. Instead, all they could do was dive back into the building as Cassady's arm was riddled with shrapnel.

"AAAGGHHH!"

Yelling in pain, Drake clutched his head, muttering, "What is going on? This has happened before!"

"DC, *are-are-are* you okay?"
Cassady let go of his heavily bleeding arm to help Drake to his feet.

Looking behind them, Cassady surveyed the scene, speaking as they walked. Drake mimicked the words under his breath, as if on autopilot.

"Looks like the entrance and exit have been shut. We'll have to find another way to move the hostages. Come on, I-I-I-I I'm not le- le- le... leaving anyone out here alone."

Drake tried to shout that this was a trap, but instead, only the words he had spoken before spilled out:
"I hear you loud and clear, CA. Let's get a move on it!"

Like a horrible play, Drake played his part as everything happened again. Just as they reached the door to the hostage room, it exploded, launching them back and embedding Drake into the wall. Ear-piercing screams snapped him awake. He watched as only the lower half of Hugh walked forward. Rose had been rocketed backward, impaled by the many state flags mounted on the conference room wall. June was the only one not killed in the blast, but her whereabouts were a mystery.

Managing to remove himself from the concrete bracings of the damaged wall, Drake shook Cassady to his feet.
"Cassady... Cassady! Wake up!"

Rubbing his forehead, Cassady took a moment to register what had happened. But the horrific expression on Drake's face said enough.

"Cassady, we have to get out of here. Most of the hostages are dead anyway. We can head back to base and radio command about the outcome."

"Fine, but first we'll need to clean up the hostages."

Almost none of the hostages had survived the explosion. The only ones left were a father and his son, knocked back from the group near Rose's body. The father covered his son trying to protect him.

Cassady walked toward them, pointing his pistol at them. Shaking in fear, the man screamed in gibberish. Rushing to Cassady's side, Drake grabbed the pistol, trying to lower it, but Cassady hit him with an unseen right hook. The hammer now free, Cassady fired, the shot striking the man's heart. His larger body fell back, pinning the boy beneath him. Cassady took a few more steps and aimed the gun at the boy's head. The child, his amber eyes wide with fear, shook back and forth to free himself, his matted blood-soaked pepper-red hair stuck to his face.

Launching like a rocket, Drake tackled Cassady to the ground, making his second shot miss. "Stop it Cassady! Everyone is dead. We can just leave!"

The two fought back and forth, exchanging blows. "*Wha- WHAT are-are-are you doing*, soldier? Never forget the mission!"

Looking into Cassady's eyes, Drake pleaded with him, "Please don't do this again! WE CAN JUST LEAVE TOGETHER! YOU DON'T HAVE TO DIE AGAIN!"

As they wrestled closer to the gun, the boy managed to free himself, pointing the weapon at the two of them. Drake raised his hands, trying to calm the child, but Cassady lunged, grabbing the gun and firing. Drake ran in front of the boy, taking the hit. Cassady then struck Drake with the pistol's handle, knocking him back.

Pg.120

Cassady's eyes were filled with the hypnotic patterns.
"*Nev- nev- never forget the job*! You know that DC!"

Drake tried to move toward Cassady, but he fired at the ground in front of him.
"I haven't, Cassady! The mission is over. We can just leave."

"Why fight me on this? *Did-did-did* you have some... something to do with this?"

"NO, Cassady! You're my friend! I would never want to hurt any of you!"

"But your mission is to clean up, and you tried to stop me! You're supposed to *PRO-PRO- PROTECT ME*!"

"It was just a man and his son! They didn't need to die; they weren't part of the politics of this nation. THEY HAD TOUR BAND TICKETS ON THEIR WRISTS!"

"It doesn't matter. They are the enemy!"

"Snap out of it, Cassady! YOU HAVE A YOUNGER BROTHER! WHAT IF THAT WAS HIM?"

Cassady's expression turned cold.
"Then I'd end that worthless enemy. All enemies of Bravati must be put down. And at this moment, you're now a worthless enemy of Bravati as well."

Pulling the gun closer to Drake's head, the hot barrel seared a mark onto his scalp.

The scene flashed, and Drake saw something different. He was kneeling in a meadow of white and red spider lilies, holding a pistol to his own head.

"Ethan?! What's going on?"

The scene flashed back, and Cassady stood before him, gun in hand.

Cassady struck Drake with the butt of the gun. "Look at me when I'm talking to you traitor!"

Drake shut his eyes, paralyzed.

"I hated you! I've always hated you. I just pretended to be nice so you'd hesitate when it mattered most. Hahaha!"

Tears streamed from Drake's eyes as he looked into Cassady's amber ones. "You don't... no!"

Cassady's twisted smile grew. "Want to know how I can top that? I ended my brother. I lied when I said I still had a brother. My parents loved him more than me. They gave everything to him for his stupid medical condition."

From the void, Ethan's voice broke through. "*Sna- sna- snap out of it Drake!*"

"So, I just moved his date up a bit. No one questioned the sad older brother sleeping in his little brother's hospital room. The only problem was the screaming. Oh well, you do what you have to survive, right, Drake?"

"Now then, let's hurry up and end this. Maybe I'll visit your brother next."

Drake's muscles tensed at the words. With a roar, he leaped at Cassady, knocking the gun away as he strangled him.

Ethan's voice grew harsher.
"DRAKE! PLEASE... STOP!"

Drake's grip loosened, and Cassady fell to the ground, gasping for air. Drake looked around wildly.
"Ethan, where are you?!"

Gasping for air, Ethan spoke,
"In front of you, big bear!"

Drake saw Cassady, but then the scene flashed again. Now, Drake stood in the meadow, Ethan lying where Cassady had been. Behind him stood a young girl, her body twisted and corrupted like the devil Drake had dealt with before.

"Hahaha! You should just stop. I can't mess with both of you at once, but your brother is already lost. KILL HIM, DRAKE!"

Ethan, his voice raw, tried to yell,
"You... little... brat! Drake! Snap... out... of... it!"

The scene flickered between the meadow and the conference room. Drake saw Cassady and Ethan both rush for the gun. Unable to risk it, Drake tackled them first.

"Drake... Please, no!"

"DO IT, DRAKE!"

The gun pointed at Cassady was also aimed at Ethan. Drake couldn't pull the trigger.

Turning, Drake saw the little boy, where the devil girl had stood. A small ball of fire rippled in their hand.

Taking aim it was pointed at both Ethan and Cassady.
Drake pleaded, but they didn't listen. Just as the small bead of fire launched, Drake shot.

A voice whispered from the void, cold and emotionless: "Good work, '*Durkin*'."

Chapter 11
Big Brother

Falling to his knees, Drake pulled Ethan into a giant hug. The two cried and laughed, holding each other tightly like true brothers once again, reunited after a long nightmare.

"Ethan, are you okay?!"

"Of course I am, you big dummy!"
Ethan chuckled, but his voice was still thick with emotion.

Drake's strength gave out as the pain from his injuries overwhelmed him. The two collapsed into the meadow of red and white spider lilies, their laughter mingling with tears as they lay side by side.

"I thought you were the one who led me here," Drake admitted, his voice cracking.

"She took your form and must have mind-controlled me, like in the movies."

"She- she- she was messing with me-me-me too."

"But I-I-I-I guess she did- did... didn't think I'd find you so soon. All my- my- my anger boiled over. I had this ma-ma-ma massive headache. Next thing I-I-I-I knew, I-I-I was near-near-near the entrance. I-I-I saw her talking to you. She-she-she said some kind of weird guttural words... Then-then-then you started calling out to Cassady. She must've been messing with our heads from the start. U-u-u-using some kind of spice or smell. She was making us angry enough to turn on e-e-e-each other."

Drake gave a small, bitter laugh.
"Well, it was working."

Ethan hesitated before speaking.
"Honestly, I-I-I-I don't think all... all of it was her."

Drake wiped Ethan's tears and placed his good hand on his brother's shoulder.
"Look, I'm sorry I left you behind, Ethan. And I'm sorry we got split up."

Ethan looked up at Drake, his expression serious.
"The splitting up part isn't your fault. They-they-they've got some kind of system... Tha-tha-that moves the rooms around the Rec House."

Drake raised an eyebrow.
"Sounds like magic or some occult stuff. Like I was saying, just turns out we are in a movie. It's been a dream of mine to be in a moving hologram show."

Ethan shot him a side eye.
"Magic isn't real Drake. And if this was a movie I got a word to say to the director!"

Drake nearly teared up at the familiar sarcasm, but Ethan shook his head firmly.
"Look-look-look, don't get too comfy. We-we still need to talk."

"We will,"
Drake promised.

Standing up, Ethan offered his hand to help his older brother.
"Okay. We better. I-I-I-I want to know what was so in-in-important that you couldn't even write too me."

Ethan struggled to support Drake, his frame just too heavy for Ethan to lift, but the two managed to start moving. Just as they left the meadow, Drake paused.

"Wait, what about the safe?"

"There wa-wa-wa-was never a safe to begin with," Ethan explained, his tone bitter.

"The little girl la-la-laughed when I asked about it. She-she... She said it was just a lure to get us here alone. We were part of some twist-twist-twisted game show."

Ethan pointed to the cameras hidden around them.

"Their indicator lights are-are broken, ba- ba- but they're still functional. They're broad-broad-broadcasting to some underground output."

"But why would they be watching us? And even more so, how did they know we were going to be here?"

"For-for-for-for the first part I-I-I'm not fully sure. They-they had put plenty of other people to slaug-slaug-slaughter... before we got here. They have recorded vid-vid-videos of it for enjoyment maybe. Like a-a-a game show, I'm not sure."

Drake's face darkened.
"So their vacation was..."

"Som-som some underground end-of-the-world party. Throw in a murder show, an-an-and I-I-I know people who'd be into it."

"Sick bastards. So, how did they know we were going to be here?"

"I'm not sure?"
Ethan threw side-eyes at Drake.

"What's that look for?"

"Cause we broke in with a rat?"

Drakes face tightened,
"Felicity would never have done that!"

Ethan looked away, for a moment, memories rushed to his mind, causing his tone to be cold and stern.
"Yeah I-I-I- I'm not so sure a-a-a- about that. Everyone turn-turn- turns on each other... Eventually."

Drake pulled Ethan's face to look at him.
"Look, I promise you she might be difficult, but she would never do that. And I'll never let her hurt you like that Ethan."

Ethan hesitated but nodded as the two continued to stand there in the rain.

Clap. Clap. Clap.

A slow, mocking applause echoed around them. The voice didn't come from behind but seemed to surround them.

"Well done Ethan."

"You might not be strong, and your thoughts on magic are flawed, but you're almost right."

From the shadows stepped a half-dressed pale green man. Unlike the devils before him, his flawless skin was covered in tattoos of an ancient language. Shimmering under the red moonlight that sat in the eye of the storm. Long, dark forest-green hair flowed past his shoulders, framed by two thick horns curving upward from his temples. His muscular frame strained against a half-vest toga skirt. Everything about him screamed power—horns, tail, hooved feet, and all.

Ethan sighed heavily.
"Not-not-not another one of you. Please, leave us a-a-a alone. We don't want any part of your game show."

The devil crouched, gently closing the young girl's barely lifeless eyes.
"Oh, but Ethan, this isn't a game. It was never about you two killing each other for money. That was just a side bet with my sister. But like you, she was too weak to know the entire plan."

The man's tattoos began to glow, a strange red energy pulsed from the man's hand. Instantly her body was consumed by a bright crimson red fire turning her to ash.

"Let me go Ethan,"
Drake growled, struggling to stand.

"your-your-your... You're in no sha-sha shape to fight," Ethan tried to hold him back.

Smiling, the devil walked closer, his tattoos glowing faintly.
"You see, we only needed Drake to start the ritual."

Drake shot the devil a furious glare.
"Cut the cult movie horror crap!"

"FEHAHAHA! It doesn't matter what you think."

Raising his left hand, it glowed a bright purple. Ethan was immediately engulfed in the same light, lifted off the ground, and hurled toward the Rec House roof with a flick of the devil's wrist.

"ETHAN! YOU BASTARD, WHAT THE HELL DID YOU DO TO ETHAN?!"

The devil scoffed, crossing his arms.
"I was only teaching him that magic is real. Here, let me show you!"

In an instant, the devil lunged at Drake with a speed that defied logic. His glowing tattoos flared a bright yellow as he drove his fist into Drake's chest, sending him hurtling through the hedge maze walls. Each impact shattered the iron bar frames in between the hedge walls. Tearing through layers of hedges until Drake skidded to a stop on the concrete patio ground of the Rec House lounge.

Blood pooled as Drake coughed violently, spitting out a bit of crimson.

"FEHAHAHA! Still breathing? Dad was right. You're the Leviathan they talked about. Any mortal would've been turned to paste from that spell."

Despite shattered ribs and a broken arm, he pushed himself up, fists raised in a boxing stance.
"Levia-who? I don't care what you call me. I'm going to kill you for what you did to Ethan!"

Pop-Pop-Pop-Pop-Pop. BOOM!

Explosions erupted all over the devil as Ethan reappeared, leaping from the patio's roof. Landing next to Drake with a small empty glass bottle in hand.

"U-u-u... You'll ha- have... to get in line big bro," Ethan grinned despite the blood trickling down the back of his head.

"I-I-I I'm not done yet."

"Ethan!"

The brothers exchanged a nod before fist bumping under the Rec House's cover.

"I was sure you got splatted somewhere."

"I-I-I I'm okay. Few-few-few broken bones but nothing tha-tha-tha that'll stop me from running. Come on, let's get... get out of here! Tha-that-that was like three frag grenades going off in your face. There's no way he's walking out of that," Ethan panted, his voice trembling as adrenaline coursed through him.

"You would be sadly mistaken again Ethan," The devil's voice called out from the smoke, a smooth yet bone-chilling tone.

"For magic is far more powerful than any technology mortals could conceive."

The devil emerged; his flawless green skin marred by deep craters from the blast. White tattoos snaked across his body like cracks in porcelain, glowing faintly with every step. As Ethan and Drake watched in horror, the wounds began to close, the flesh knitting together until the devil's body was whole once more.

"How- how- how the hell are u-u-u you doing that?!" Ethan demanded; his voice tinged with disbelief.

"I-I-I I've nev-nev never heard of a device tha-tha-tha that could do that!"

"It's not some simple device, Ethan." The devil gave a mocking grin.

"It's magic—the most powerful thing in existence."

The devil raised his left hand, conjuring a small, swirling bead of fire. With a flick, he sent it toward the hedge wall behind himself. It erupted into a towering inferno. The ground shook and the air shimmered with blistering heat, the rain boiling into a thick mist. The brothers could do nothing but stare, their faces pale with disbelief.

"You see, those who wield magic are the most powerful beings in existence. With magic, you can reshape reality, bend others to your will, or obliterate entire cities."

Ethan gritted his teeth.
"Then-then why don't u-u-u you just take control of us now an-an-an and get it over with?"

The devil smirked.
"Astute question. Magic has its rules, and I am bound by them, just as you are bound by your ignorance. However..."

He tilted his head, his glowing tattoos pulsing faintly. "It's even more hilarious that you can't even tell that you've crafted magic yourself. Your little device? It's more magical than you realize."

"What?"
Ethan narrowed his eyes.

The devil continued;
"The crystal inside vibrates to link with the caster
network. But when you broke it, you transformed it
when you put it back together. And it became
something special. You didn't just modify a
bracelet, Ethan—you built your own caster-net
station. That's why we can't manipulate it. And in
turn stop you from digging your holes in our
network. Brilliant work, though completely
unintentional. If only father & my other siblings
could see your mind like I could. Then we wouldn't
have thrown such weaklings against you. "

Ethan's eyes widened in disbelief.
"Wait... you're saying I-I-I-I accidentally made...
magic? Tha-tha-tha that's impossible, I-I-I-I don't
even believe in the crap. I just happened to fix a
device with a few simple mod... Modifications."

"Magic doesn't care what you believe in. It simply
is."
"ETHAN DON'T!"
Drake shouted, but Ethan's hand was already in his
backpack.

"How- how- how about I-I-I show you what kind-
kind-kind kind of devices I make. Tha-tha-tha
Than you'll know what I-I-I-I believe in!"

He pulled out a hawk-shaped drone lined with gray
clay. Tossing it into the air, he piloted it toward the
devil with a handheld controller.

"FEHAHAHA! What you believe in is flawed,"
The devil's left-hand glowed with a hue that looked
like he had pulled a piece of outer space out from
the galaxy above. Containing a multitude of stars, it
moved like a liquid in his hand, but he held it like a
solid.

The drone exploded in a fiery eruption, but then the blast instantly collapsed into an orb of the same material that the devil held. In seconds, the hawk reappeared, whole and untouched. The devil flicked it away as if it were a mere nuisance, sending it hurtling far into the distance.

Ethan dropped to his knees, his hands trembling. "That... that was my strongest weapon."

"Now do you see?"
Stepping closer, his wings unfurling behind him like a shadow consuming the storm above, as it's fury returned to the lands. Each beat sent a gust of wind that shook the ground beneath them.

"The game was rigged from the start."

Drake grabbed Ethan, pulling him to his feet. "Snap out of it, Ethan! Don't let him get in your head!"

Ethan flinched as Drake slapped him across the face. "OW! Wa-wa-wa What the hell?!"

"Out of the moment, Ethan!"
Drake shouted, his voice cracking with desperation.

"YOU NEED TO RUN!"

Tears streamed down Ethan's face.

"NO! We-we-we still hav- hav- haven't talked yet! There's still... so much I-I-I-I need to say to you!"

"It's too late for that! You remember mom! Just go, this time don't call the police. JUST RUN!"

"Ba-ba-ba But Drake!"

Pg.135

"SHUT UP ETHAN, JUST RUN!"
Drake roared, the beast from within peering out
from Drake's eyes.

The devil took advantage of the distraction, driving
a bone-bending punch into Drake's chest. As Drake
crumpled, gasping for air, the devil turned to strike
Ethan. But Drake caught the blow with his good
hand, his knuckles cracking from the force.

"You're not laying another finger on my little bro!"
Drake snarled. With a roar, he headbutted the devil.
The impact staggered the creature for a moment,
but his cruel grin only widened.

"You have spirit, Leviathan. I'll enjoy breaking it."

"ETHAN, RUN!"
Drake bellowed.

So he did. He burst through the Rec House doors,
sprinting past half-constructed roads and familiar
landmarks. But then he stopped, gasping for air.
His mind screamed for him to keep going, but his
heart wouldn't let him.

He could still hear Drake's laugh, feel the reassuring
weight of his hand on his shoulder. And then he
remembered the years of silence, the unanswered
questions.

"{No more running,}"

"{If this was the end, then I'd face it together with
my brother.}"

Turning back toward the Rec House, Ethan froze as he saw it—a monstrous silhouette against the stormy sky. The devil's leathery wings stretched impossibly wide, their jagged edges glinting like shattered glass in the lightning. Each beat sent a thunderous crack through the air, shaking the ground beneath his feet.

Ethan's legs screamed for him to run. But not this time. Not when Drake was still out there, he had to live for the two of them, to save his older brother.

"YOU SHOULD HAVE RAN AWAY LITTLE RAT! THE CHASE DIDN'T NEED TO END SO SOON!"

Chapter 12
Ethan

Pant... pant...

SPLASH-SPLASH-SPLASH!

"YOU CAN'T HIDE FOREVER!"
The devil's voice boomed, echoing like thunder across the unfinished construction site.

FHOOOM!

Another explosion rattled the air, sending debris cascading into the downpour.
"I'll find you eventually little rat! This decaying construction won't hide you for long."

Ethan crouched low in the shadow of the crumbling wall, his breath coming in ragged gasps.

"{Crap!-Crap!-Crap! What the heck am I going to do? There's no way I can get past this guy and make it back to Drake without being seen. And fighting him? No. Not long range, not medium range...}"
He glanced at his scrawny frame.

"And definitely not close-range."

His trembling hand brushed against a jagged piece of metal. His body ached with exhaustion, and tears stung his eyes.

"{Why the hell did I have to get dragged into this? I just wanted the money. I didn't need Drake crashing back into my life, making me forgive him. I was fine on my own. Granite City would've been better alone...}"

The storm quieted for a moment, leaving only the sound of rain splattering against broken concrete.

Ethan gritted his teeth.
"{You'd better still be alive Drake.}"

Summoning his courage, Ethan peeked through the broken window. His heart nearly stopped. On the other side of the shattered frame, the devil stood, his glowing white tattoos twisting like snakes under his skin. His flawless green body glistened in the rain, the faint crimson-gold aura shimmering around him.

"Found you little rat!"

"QWACK!"

Ethan ducked back down, scrambling through the tunnel of fallen construction supplies. Behind him, the devil's aura flared, and the wall Ethan had been hiding behind exploded into rubble.

The devil advanced, the glow around him deflecting flying debris. A small object; some kind of puffer fish, puffed up with spikes as it collided with the barrier. Bursting into a spray of needles that bounced harmlessly off the shield, it's yellow fog seeped through. The devil didn't notice as he inhaled some of it. Instantly he began to cough up blood, he staggered back from the toxic cloud.

"Hah! You like that? That-that-that's my Chloro-Spike Puffer Fish. Nasty needles, ba-ba-but the smoke's the real kicker."

Pg.139

More puffer fish fell from the rafters above, bursting into even more needles and choking yellow gas. Ethan grinned as he struck a match, flicking it into the cloud.

"U-u-u You wanna know why I-I-I-I wanted you to come inside? Because this part doesn't work in the rain."

BOOOOOOOM!

The explosion tore through the building, blowing it apart in a fiery inferno. Ethan barely escaped, tumbling out of the structure as the shockwave sent him skidding across the muddy ground. His body ached from the impact, rocks scraping his skin. Coughing, he looked up, praying it was over.

Through the smoke, a shadow emerged. The concrete slab stood intact, and there, bathed in golden light, the devil stepped forward.

"{Are you kidding me?!}"

The devil's voice rang out, calm and unbothered. "You mortals are so clever... and so foolish. FEHAH HA HA HA. You think a little explosion like that would hurt me? Did I not teach you at the hedge maze-"

The smirk on his face faltered as he staggered back, clutching his head and stomach. Suddenly, he vomited a considerable amount of blood. His skin and eyes began to take on a sickly yellow hue.

"The air you're in is still poisonous, idi-idi-idiot!" Ethan shouted, a mixture of fear and defiance in his voice, as he stood quickly retreating.

The devil straightened up, his expression hardening. "You shouldn't have told me that."

Twisting his hands in complex gestures, he formed several glowing hand signs. His body was engulfed in a radiant white light, the yellow hue draining from his skin and eyes. Whipping his hands outward, three small ebony spheres materialized, hovering ominously. With a flick of his wrist, the spheres transformed into beams of necrotic energy, rocketing toward Ethan.

Turning just in time to see the beams, Ethan was unable to dodge completely. He rolled, narrowly avoiding two of them. But as he shot back into a sprint, the third beam struck his left arm's elbow. Instantly, an infectious pain tore through his arm. His elbow felt as if it were aging and rotting in mere seconds. Rainwater hit the wound, washing away flakes of skin and muscle. The agony was so overwhelming that it forced Ethan to crumble to the ground in pain. His landing was rough, the impact snapping his left humerus. The bone withered under the strain, separating most of his left arm from his body.

"AAAHHH!"

Clutching the remains of his arm, Ethan fumbled for a rag, tying it tightly around the stump to staunch the bleeding and shield the wound. Tears streamed down his face, but he clenched his jaw and forced himself to focus.

"GET- UP! FIGHT!"

Ethan roared to himself through gritted teeth. "{It doesn't matter how much it hurts. I have to live for the two of us!}"

Before he could act, he was yanked from the ground, the devil lifting him effortlessly into the air. Ethan dangled helplessly; his body wracked with pain.

"You've proven to be a crafty little rat Ethan!"

"Taking out three Iron-Jaw Wildebeest Pups by yourself and surviving the traps my little brother set. Impressive, but ultimately futile."

The devil muttered a string of arcane words, as his claws sank deep into Ethan's sides. A searing blue light erupted from his hands, causing Ethan's body to convulsed violently as electricity surged through him.

"SHOCKING, ISN'T IT?"

"AAAAHHHHH!!!"
The pain was unbearable.

"Magic is wondrous, is it not?"
The devil pumped another surge of electricity into Ethan before soaring into the stormy sky.

"FEHAH HA HA HA! PITIFUL MORTAL! I CAN'T WAIT TO WATCH YOU SPLAT LIKE YOUR BROTHER! I CAN ALWAYS RECOVER YOUR BRAIN LATER! NOW DIE LIKE THE PITIFUL WORM YOU ARE!"

As the devil dropped him, time seemed to slow as Ethan's mind raced frantically. The world around him blurred, and he caught sight of something in the storm. A glint of light. It was his H.A.W.K. drone, circling like a silent sentinel. His eyes panned to a wind vane atop a distant building.

"I'LL SHOW YOU WHAT'S SHOCKING!"
Ethan roared! His mind snapping into focus.

Reaching into his backpack with his left hand, he retrieved a small grappling gun. With a shaky aim, he fired toward the nearby wind vane. As the hook snagged onto its base rod, Ethan clutched the gun to his chest, flipping the switch to retract it. The mechanism pulled him into a wide arc as bolts of fire shot from the devil's fingertips, narrowly missing him.

Ethan swung high, the momentum carrying him over the mansion, but it forced him to crash into the walls of its widow's walk. He hit the structure hard, his back slamming against the iron railings. Pain coursed through his battered body, and all he could do was lay there, gasping for air.

The devil descended; his face twisted with fury. "How many times must I keep teaching you this?!"

Coughing up blood, Ethan smirked weakly. "Sorr- sorry, I- I- I didn't catch that. Wha- wha- what did you say?!"

"Your gadgets only delay the inevitable! I WILL KILL YOU!"
Electricity crackled in his hands as he lunged toward Ethan.

"Wait for it..."
Ethan muttered under his breath, flipping the switch on the drone's remote.

The H.A.W.K. drone soared high into the air before diving straight at the devil. The resulting explosion was deafening, the force slamming the devil into the sharp iron railings of the widow's walk. The pointed ends pierced his wings and shoulders, pinning him in place.

The devil struggled, his body wiggling as he pulled against the bars. Sparks of lightning gathered around his hands, but he couldn't free himself.

"Stuck, huh?"
Ethan quipped, struggling to his feet.

The devil writhed and pulled against the bars again, his eyes blazing with hatred.
"YOU WON'T ESCAPE ME!"

"Huh? That doesn't sound shocking enough. You know what's shocking? Putting iron on your roof."
Ethan reached into his backpack, pulling out a beetle-shaped robot. He cracked its horn causing the beetle's blue wings to buzz to life.

"It's like these houses were just asking for lightning to strike them."

Ethan tossed the beetle at the devil. Sparks of electricity erupted around him, intensifying as the storm above mirrored the chaos. Lightning gathered into a massive charge, culminating in a blinding explosion that engulfed the devil entirely.
"That's the shocking part."

BOOOOOOOOOOMMMM!!!

Ethan staggered, his vision swimming with black dots and flashes of light. He clutched his side, his strength failing.

"Alright, Drake, I-I- I'm... on my way,"
Collapsing onto the cold, rain-soaked roof.

"{NO! DRAKE NEeds... me...}"
Slipping away, the storm's fury continued to rage on.

Pg.144

Chapter 13
Drake

"Aaahhh!"

Drake strikes the devil across the face, knocking him back a few more feet.

"I will never let you pass me!!"

"I commend the might, but this Mountain is already crumbling."

Catching Drake's next swing, the devil reached out and grabbed Drake's mangled hand. Snapping Drake's wrist, he cut it clean off with his bladed fingers. Yelling out in pain, Drake took a few steps backward but then Drake was pulled into the devil's arms. Feeling a sharp, warm pain enter his gut. Blood rained from the sky as the two rose in the air, their embrace one of pain and of love.

"You may not know this now, but you were truly a monster. A creature that rivaled the ancient split mountains in size. What they have done to you is hateful. What I have done to you is a kindness. But before I finish, I must break your weak shell. My father's plans for you are almost to fruition."

Speaking into the wind, the devil had not noticed that Drake had already lost consciousness, "FEHAH Ha ha ha!! Here I go wasting time. I must not upset father."

Pg.145

WwwwhhHHHOOOOOSSSSHHH... ...THUD

Flash

Ambulance sirens blare off in the background.

"Drake, can you shut the window? Your mother just got done complaining. I don't want another loud useless sound screeching in my ears."

The woman hisses at the man,
"Shut the hell up, Jackson!"

A young boy jumped out of the chair much larger than him, his shaggy black hair bouncing up and down as he walked.

SLAM

"DRAKE!"

The young boy pulled his hands up over his face,
"I'm sorry, sir."

The man sighed and drank from his smuggled-in bottle of booze.

"Are you kidding me Jackson!"

"What? I needed something for all your yelling and complaining!"

Drake's mother handed over her newly delivered baby to the nurse. Taking the child, they laid the little one on the baby care cart, walking away to avoid the volatile couple. However, once he put the baby down, it began to cry. His parents still caught up in their fight, paid no mind to Drake as he moved over picking the baby up.

Locking eyes with him, Drake smiled.
"So you're my little brother?"

He poked the baby's belly, causing it to smile and laugh, wiggling in his arms.

Walking back into the room, the nurse just laid the birth certificate on the baby care table, not wanting to get involved in the couple's chaos.

"Mommy, mommy, the nurse brought in some papers."

But she didn't hear him, instead screaming at the top of her lungs, causing the baby to cry again.

"There she goes again! Not getting your way, so you have a tantrum!"

Stepping back, Drake took the infant and the paperwork out into the hallway. He set the baby down on a few chairs next to the door into his mother's room. Poking its belly again until it would smile..

"HHHMMM... what are we going to name you? Bruce?"

He looked at the infant. "Nah, that's not right. Kevin?"

The baby didn't seem so happy hearing that name.

"Hhhhmmm, OH! ETHAN! That's it. I had a really cool friend named that once, but he's gone now. You look a lot like him too. That's it. I'll name you Ethan!"

The baby began to cheer and giggle at the name, "Yep, that settles it, ha haha ha."
Picking the baby back up, Drake hugged his new brother Ethan tightly.

Flash

VVRroommm!....

A broken woman sat in the kitchen. Her mangled, greasy chocolate hair lay over her scarred face. Tears dripped from her blackened eye into a trembling glass of whiskey.

"Mom! Dad is leaving. What did I do?"
A young Ethan, parting the tears from his eyes while also trying not to get the document in his hand wet.

The woman stopped shaking seeing that the paper in Ethan's hand was a DNA heritage test.

"I'm sorry, Mom. Drake took me to the mall last month, and I snuck away."

The woman rose her whiskey glass in the air, throwing it at Ethan. However, Drake rushed in, catching it at the last moment.

"Does it make you feel bigger?... Hitting someone else after what he did to you?"
Drake's face filled with anger, his blood boiling. Though he was only fourteen, he stood as if he were already a man.

"If you're going to think about hitting anyone, blame me for not watching him closer!"

Crack!

The whiskey glass burst in his hand.

"And if you're going to hit me, then I'm ready to fight you back. You're nowhere near as scary as Jackson!"

Pg.148

Looking back at her, his brown eyes had shifted to blue. The air changed, as if Drake were releasing a monster that had been locked within him to show its teeth. At this moment, it was as if his mother was a rabbit, and the thing she gave birth too was a wolf.

"At least I can be certain that you're Jackson's! You're a monster just like him!"

The woman fell back in her chair, tears falling from her eyes as she slammed her body on the dining table, flailing and screaming as she flung her arms around.

"Come on, Ethan."
Drake took him out of the kitchen and into their shared bedroom.

Pat .. Pat .. Pat

Pulling him in, Drake locked the bedroom door behind the two of them.
"I'm sorry, Drake. I didn't mean to . . ."

Drake looked at him,
"You didn't do anything wrong to be honest. I didn't think you'd even be able to ask for something like this. You are really smart, Ethan. Why didn't' you come to me with this first."

"I-I-I I'm sorry, Drake! I-I-I wanted to know if I wa-wa-was related to the people in the history books. My- my- friend said he was related to so many... many different historic people. So- so- I lied to the guy at the stall an-an-and said dad told me to get it."

Drake put his hand on Ethan's head, "It's okay. It's going to be okay, little man. Jackson isn't your real father, and it looks like he didn't like finding that out. I doubt many guys would, but he was an ass, so who cares? At this moment, you're still my little brother."

Flash

KKSSSSSSHHHHHHHHH!

A whisky bottle flew across the living room and shattered against the wall. The acrid scent of spilled alcohol filled the air, mingling with the tense silence that followed.

"I said never to look at me, you horrible mistake!" she screamed, her voice ragged and venomous.

Ethan tensed, curling inward to the corner of the living room. His small frame seemed to shrink further under her glare.

"I-I-I-I I'm sor- sor- sorry. It wa- wa- was... A mis- mis- mistake."

"Speak normal, god dammit! Why am I paying for those classes if you're so damn smart?"
Her words lashed at him like a whip.

"I'm sorry Mom ... I'll try harder,"
Ethan stammered, his voice trembling.

"How many times have I told you—"

She lurched forward; her face twisted with fury.
"I'M NOT YOUR MOTHER!"

She rose from her chair, knocking it over in her drunken rage. Her movements were erratic, unsteady, as she lunged toward Ethan. But before she could reach him, Drake barreled into her, tackling her to the ground.

"Don't you dare!" Drake shouted, his voice shaking with both fear and fury. He tried to pin her down, but she clawed at his face, leaving deep, jagged cuts.

"GET OFF ME!"

She shrieked, thrashing violently. Her knee slammed into Drake's stomach, knocking the wind out of him, and her fist connected with his jaw.

"AAAGHH! Ethan, go to the neighbors and call the cops!"

Ethan hesitated by the front door, his hand hovering over the knob. The sound of their struggle froze him in place. Then he heard it, Drake's scream. Turning back, he saw the glint of metal in her hand. The dirty steak knife drove into Drake's side, the blade sinking deep.

"I SAID GET OFF ME!" she screamed again, her voice a cacophony of anger and despair.

"Mom?!"

"DRAKE!" Ethan's cry tore through the room.

"Stay back!" Drake managed to gasp, clutching the knife embedded in his side.

"Get the cops. Now!"

"Ba-ba-ba- ba- But—"

"JUST GO GET HELP! I'LL BE FINE!"
Drake roared, his face twisted in pain and
determination.

Drake grabbed her wrists, keeping the knife lodged
in his side to stop her from using it again. Leaning
back, he smashed his forehead into hers. She
staggered, dazed, giving Drake the moment he
needed to pull the knife free.

"Finally snapped, huh?"
he muttered through gritted teeth, his breaths
labored.

She stumbled back, clutching her head, tearing at
her hair.
"You monsters have destroyed my life! I was
beautiful before you two. Men wanted me! I didn't
live in a trash dump! I was with high society! BUT
YOU LEECHES DRAGGED ME DOWN, JUST
LIKE JACKSON!"

Drake's expression darkened.
"You mean my father."

Her scream reached a pitch that made the windows
tremble. She lunged at him again, but this time,
Drake swung his fist. The force of the blow lifted
her off her feet and sent her crashing into the wall,
shattering glass and whisky alike.

Moments later, the wail of police sirens grew louder, filling the tense silence as they arrived to take her away.

Soon the sirens faded into the distance as the police lifters disappeared into the sky. Drake emerged from the house, bandaged and bruised, carrying an icepack in one hand. He dropped onto the porch steps beside Ethan, who sat silently, his eyes swollen from crying.

"Hey, you okay little man?"
Drake's voice soft despite the pain.

Ethan didn't answer. Instead, he threw his arms around Drake, clinging to him.

Drake winced but managed a weak smile.
"Alright, let's clean up that nose, okay?"

Ethan nodded, flinching as the rag touched his face.

"Hold the ice with the rag. It'll hurt less,"
Drake smiled faintly.

Ethan did as he was told, sniffing through his tears. "I-I-I- I-I I'm sor-sor-sorry"

"It's okay little man. She barely hurt me, but I want you to know that you can say whatever's on your mind. Even if it's hard. I'll listen."

Ethan's lip quivered, and more tears spilled over. He dropped the rag & icepack. Wrapping his arms around Drake again.

Drake hugged him back, his gaze shifting toward the horizon as if ensuring they were truly alone.

"Listen, Ethan,"

"We've gotta stick together now. If we don't, we won't make it. You're the brains. You've got a lot going for you, and I'm not letting that die. I'll live for the two of us, okay?"

Flash

"Drake... Drake! Wake up!"

{Wait, what's going on?}
Rubbing his forehead, it took Drake a moment to register what had happened. But the horrific expression on Cassady's face said enough.

"Drake, we have to get out of here. Most of the hostages are dead anyway. We can just head back to the base and radio command about the outcome."

"Fine, but first we'll need to clean up the hostages."

Among the scattered bodies, only a father and his son had survived the explosion. The father had shielded the boy with his own body, now lying atop the child. The boy's small, terrified form trembled beneath him.

Drake moved forward, pistol in hand, pointing it at the two.

{This isn't how it happened.}

The man screamed in Hasprin, his voice cracking with desperation.
"Torma- 'ercein 'solerc soltor- 'einriterc umisol"

Cassady rushed to Drake's side, his hand reaching for the pistol.
"Drake, stop!"

But Drake struck him with a sudden, unseen right hook, sending him stumbling backward. Freed from restraint, Drake took the shot, the bullet slamming into the father's chest.

The man's body fell heavily, pinning the boy beneath him. The child squirmed and struggled, but his father's weight kept him trapped. Drake advanced, his gun now trained on the boy's head. The boy's amber eyes locked on the barrel, wide with terror. He twisted and fought, his matted red pepper hair streaked with dirt and blood, but his movements only tangled him further.

Cassady launched himself at Drake, tackling him to the ground before he could fire. Knocking the gun to the ground.

"Stop it, Drake! Everyone is dead—we can just leave!"

The two men grappled, exchanging punches, each blow laced with desperation.

"What are you doing, soldier?!"
Drake snarled, his voice cold and unyielding.

"Never forget the mission!"

Cassady's voice broke, pleading as he met Drake's unrelenting gaze.
"We can just leave together! You don't have to do this! They are just normal people, look at their tour bands."

Pg.155

Their struggle grew more frenzied as they fought for control of the gun. The young boy managed to free himself in the chaos, grabbing the discarded weapon. Shaking, he pointed it at the two men, his small frame trembling with rage and fear.

"Stop!"
the boy screamed, his voice cracking.

Cassady raised his hands, stepping back cautiously.

"It's okay, kid. We're not going to hurt you,"

But Drake, with a sudden burst of force, lunged at the boy. He wrenched the gun from his small hands, turning it in one swift motion.
"No!"
Cassady roared, rage and anguish overtaking him.

BANG!

Drake turned the gun on Cassady without hesitation, unloading two shots into his left leg. Cassady collapsed, groaning in pain, his body writhing on the ground.

Stepping forward, his boot pressing down on Cassady's chest, pinning him. He raised the gun, its barrel pointed squarely at Cassady's face.

BANG!

"Never forget the mission, soldier,"
Drake's voice devoid of emotion, his eyes were filled with hypnotic patterns.

Chapter 14
Ethan

THOOM!

"DRAKE!!"

{Crap! How long have I been out? I've got to get up! AAAHHH! Crap, my hip—I must've torn it again when I hit the iron bars.}

Ethan shot awake, yelling his brother's name. His eyes darted around the widow's walk; the smoldering ashes of the devil now reduced to a sloppy puddle. He didn't give it a second thought. Gritting his teeth, he tried to rocket up, but the stabbing pain in his hip slowed him down. Frantically searching his backpack, he found the shattered bottle of pain meds, their contents scattered in the yard below.

"No-no-no-no-no!"
Yanking at his hair.

Pulling himself upright, leaning heavily on the iron railing for support. He walked over to the nearby exit. Slamming his shoulder into the door, he pushed his way inside.

Blood dripped from his hip & missing left arm, leaving a trail behind him as he stumbled down the stairs. His fingers clutched at the walls, desperate for balance, until he found the front door. Ethan yanked it open, the force of which knocking him back onto the floor.

"{GET UP DAMMIT!}"

Dizzy from blood loss and exhaustion, he froze. A stunning young woman appeared in the doorway; her face shrouded by a veil of light. She reached out her hand, and though Ethan hesitated, he grabbed it. Her touch was warm, and familiar. Tears welled in his eyes as his mouth moved, trying to speak, but she silenced him with a gentle kiss to his lips. She tapped his forehead lightly.

"Go get him Wires."

"Please, don't go!"
Ethan pleaded, his voice cracking.

She didn't answer, only turning him toward the Rec House, giving him a firm push. By the time Ethan turned back, she was gone.

His hand instinctively found the charm in his pocket, his fingers brushing over Kat's initials scrawled on the back. He nodded silently, a newfound energy surging through him. The pain in his hip dulled just enough for him to start running again.

As he sprinted toward the Rec House, doubt crept into his thoughts.

{More magic, huh? Maybe it's true. Or maybe it's technology i just don't understand yet. I like that idea better.}

THOOOOMMM

Lightning races overhead as Ethan reached the front doors of the Rec House. Pulling up his c-net bracelet light he scanned the room. Taking out Drake's keys, Ethan unlocked the doors slipping inside.

Pg.158

"Drake! Drake!"

"{You better be okay.}"

But Drake didn't answer. His heart clenched as he ran past the chandelier's remains, only to find a small impact crater covered in blood. His brother's body was missing. Cold dread washed over him as he spotted a trail of blood leading behind the service desk.

Following it, he pushed through the dual doors, weaving through the maze of hallways until he reached Timothy Cherrywood's office once again.

It's trail now traveled across the room, further past the left open oil painting. Ethan stepped through, his footsteps echoing on the metal floor. Ahead, a thick steel door loomed, it was marked with Gale-Wind Steel Manufacturing's insignia. The hermetically sealed door had a 36-digit passcode lock & reinforced titanium bolts lining its frame. "{Ha, Child's play!}"

Ethan dropped his backpack; he didn't hesitate as he pulled out his tools. He connected the badger box to the keypad with several different colored wires. Popping a flash drive into the keypad he flicked the device on, his 8-bit badger appeared on the screen, digging through the code. In moments, the lock disengaged with a loud

CLUNK,

And the vaults door swung free.

The sight inside froze him in his tracks. Lining the walls of the lab were vats containing mutilated bodies. Stripped of their skin and patched with leathery flesh, their heads were grotesquely misshapen to give them horns. Some had their eyes and tongues removed, while others had them replaced with bizarre, tattooed versions.

The air reeked of chemicals and decay. The vats bubbled faintly, the sound a grotesque mockery of life. Ethan's mind filling with anger as he stepped further inside, his light revealing a severed hand floating in a lone tank.
Near the center of the room, several operating tables stood empty—except for one. Ethan approached it, his heart sinking as he inspected the mess of blood and flesh left behind.

"{This has to be Drake's blood,}"
Ethan's mind raced.

"{What the hell did they do to you, big bear?}"

In the far corner of the lab, he discovered a hidden door. Inside was a smaller workspace filled with trinkets, a computer, chemical supplies, and mechanical parts. Among the trinkets was a necklace made of bone beads, each sparking with a faint glow when touched. He pocketed it, thinking of the older devil's magic.

A twisted white stick wrapped in barbed wire caught his eye, along with a prosthetic hand made of an unfamiliar dark metal. Its knuckles were embedded with gems similar to the necklace's beads.

"*{Magic, my ass. This must be how they're faking magic. These gems must vibrate at a certain frequency. That's how they're powering their devices. Just like how the bracelets vibrate. Magic, huh? Looks like I know how to be the most powerful now.}*"

Using the strange materials, Ethan constructed a prosthetic arm to replace the one he'd lost. He outfitted it with a blade, a grappling gun, a small shield, and a taser in the palm. The first finger and thumb became a makeshift crossbow. *{No time to test it now. I have to find Drake.}*

Sliding into the computer chair, Ethan powered up the system. A familiar badger appeared on the screen, chewing through the password box. Once inside, he scanned the files, his fingers trembling as he uncovered horrifying details.

The documents outlined a project involving the surgical modification of humans into monstrous soldiers. One file caught his eye:

"*Subject SHM-011: Mountain Leviathan – Prototype Complete.*"

"Leviathan..."
Ethan whispered, his blood running cold.

Entering a greater grounded secondary connection from Timothy's PC to the main network of the park. Ethan navigated to the boards' networking system, tracing back to the servers connected to the Blood Moons Harvest. Scanning through the files, he noted instructions for Badger to continue devouring unlocked data across all networks.

The badger popped its head out of a hole made in the screensaver, tilting its head with a curious look.

"[It may take several stops to the den to upload the copied data,]"
Its text appearing on the screen.

"[Not a problem. I've already routed you a tunnel from Ethan's caster-net to act as an expressway,]"
Ethan typed back, his fingers flying over the keyboard.
The badger grinned and pawed at the screen.

"[Thank you so much, papa. You are the greatest papa in the whole world.]"
It disappeared back into its hole, leaving Ethan to continue his work.

Sigh!

"{This sucks. I can watch a live broadcast, but I can't go back. I hate to say this, but I wish they were recording this. Since their just broadcasting to other projectors. Hmm... maybe I can connect to the cameras and act like another projector and see if I can find out where they took Drake from here.}"

Sliding several tabs aside, Ethan pulled out another flash drive. Inserting it into the black box, the screen flickered, revealing numerous camera feeds.

"{With this strong connection I should be able to get all the channels.}"

Cycling through the different underground cameras, Ethan spotted Anthony and Lincoln Campbell fighting each other, while Baillie and Felicity Campbell were being chased by a massive ogre like that in fantasy books.

"{Well, at least it's good to know we aren't the only ones dealing with this crap. When I sell this to the news, I'll have a few voices backing me up—and they wouldn't mind a few extra thousand dollars. From what I looked up your family is just as messed up as mine.}"

Ethan winced as his gaze caught Felicity falling and getting snatched up by the ogre. For a moment, hope filled him. But Baillie knocked over a massive granite statue, toppling it onto the creature and freeing Felicity.

"{Oh well, a man can dream,}"
Ethan sighed, his thoughts briefly wandering.

He shook his head, snapping back to focus. "{Alright, quit messing around. Drake's in trouble, and he's not on any of these screens. Maybe I should try the Moon Lit Blood Room? With a name like that it's basically a daycare.}"

Typing into the keyboard, Ethan used the same password from before to unlock the main screen. The display shifted to tunnel feeds.

Cycling through them, he saw figures clad in dark red and black robes, the emblem of a flaming horned crown emblazoned on their chests.

Ethan's expression grew annoyed, "{Great, more magic devil nuts. Like roaches under the fridge—you never know how many are hiding.}"

Some of the robed figures had grotesque body augmentations similar to the devils Ethan had encountered earlier. Among them, others bore brighter red robes, carrying ornate daggers with twisted serpent-like designs, handles made from a ebony crystal.

"{There has to be a camera showing Drake,}"

Finally, he found the main camera used for the broadcast. It captured a massive stone coliseum filled with devils in the audience. In the arena below, a malformed creature was locked in combat with two ogres.
The monstrous figure was imposing, standing over nine feet tall. Sharp, octopus-like tentacles sprouted from its back, lifting the two ogres. With a sickening crack, it snapped one ogre's neck, discarding it's lifeless body. The monster then sprinted towards the other restrained ogre, leaping onto it with terrifying agility. Its massive jaws tore into the ogre's neck, ripping a grotesque flap of flesh. As the ogre screamed in agony, clutching its bleeding throat, the creature devoured the chunk of flesh whole. Its tentacles retracted into its back as it slapped its belly and let out a feral roar, the sound echoing like that of a beast from a twisted carnival.

The crowd erupted into a cacophony of cheers, claps, and snaps.

"[DID YOU SEE THAT, FOLKS?! What a wondrous display from the ONE, the LEGEND... THE MOUNTAIN LEVIATHAN!!]"
Boomed a voice from the speakers, igniting an even louder uproar from the crowd.

The announcer continued,
"[But that's not all! Soon, he will be reunited with his LOVE and his KILLER!!]"

The crowd's cheers intensified.
"[WATCH as we reenact the TEARS of the DEVIL QUEEN'S TALE!]"

Ethan's eyes darted between the camera feeds, his heart sinking. The monstrous figure in the center dragged a slain ogre to the middle of the arena, tearing into its corpse.

Ethan's hand trembled,
"Wait... Leviathan? No... THAT'S DRAKE!!"

Chapter 15
Drake

The sound of medical equipment coming to life echoed throughout the cold, sterile room.

"Grab the surgical tools from the cabinet near the vats. It would seem that none of my idiot offspring can follow a single task,"
A Voice commanded.

Another voice, timid and hesitant, interrupted.
"In all fairness, your Lordship, it was two tasks. And no one thought the other boy capa—"

The words were cut short as the speaker let out a blood-curdling scream. The sound of tearing flesh and a torrent of blood splattering the walls and floor filled the room.

"Clean this up! I will retrieve the surgical tools myself," The Voice barked, his tone dripping with disdain.

A feminine voice quickly obeyed. Chanting a few words and wiggling her fingers, she made the mess vanish as if it had never been.

"Good, now step away from the specimen. You pups have no idea who we have in our mitts. Your Underhands have returned to us Master! I will guide them back to your loving flame!"

Pg.166

The feminine voice hesitated but dared to speak. "I have obtained the clockwork heart you requested, Master Timothy, sir."

Timothy raised his hand slightly, silencing her immediately. She let out a hushed squeal but continued, standing rigid and terrified.

"I placed it on the tray beside the tools."

"Good, good!"
Timothy's tone shifting to an unsettling glee.

Turning back to Drake's body, Timothy gathered the surgical tools. Like a macabre performer, he juggled the sharp instruments with unsettling precision. Moving with unnatural grace, he danced around Drake's body, making calculated incisions with surgical mastery. The first long slice across the sternum revealed Drake's chest cavity. With a flick of his forceps, Timothy exposed Drake's metallic rib cage.

Carefully removing his damaged organs, he replaced them with newly modified works of art brought to him by his assistant. Suturing him back up, Timothy began to chant. Beams of white light burst from his hands raining down on Drake. In moments Drake gasped for air; he was alive but not functional.

"As I thought!"

One of his assistants dared to speak.
"Great work, Master Timothy, but what about his brain? He's been without oxygen for over 15 minutes. Hypoxia would have—"

Timothy raised his hand again, and the assistant recoiled, cowering on the floor. Tears streamed down her face as she braced for a punishment that didn't come. Instead, Timothy leaned down, placing a hand on her shoulder.

"Sir?"

Timothy placed his other hand over Drake's head. A white glow enveloped the man's skull.

"You're right; hypoxia caused some damage. But he'll be fine. The enhancements I've implanted will keep him functional even if his brain is compromised. Still, I'd prefer not to present my Master with a vegetable."

The assistant flinched as she stood up.
"Do you also plan to outfit him with an adamantine skeleton?"

Timothy's expression darkened. Moving his hand over her abdomen, his fingers glowed with a sinister purple light. The assistant's body convulsed as bolts of electricity coursed through her, the screams echoing in the sterile room. Timothy dropped her crumpled form to the floor without a second glance.

"Simpleton, I already have."

Timothy turned back to Drake, his gaze softening into something disturbingly affectionate. His gloved hands caressed Drake's chest and arms, his voice lowering to a whisper.

"Just like in the military, you endure punishment unlike any other. The fools who created you. Those imbeciles thought they built true potential. But I did. Oh, I did."

His hands trailing over Drake's chest and arms.

"You never questioned your strength, did you? Never wondered why you could endure so much? You thought it was their experiments or your sheer willpower... but no. I designed you for this."

He chuckled, his gloved fingers lingering over Drake's wrist.
"Let's fix this blemish."

Walking to one of the vats, Timothy typed commands into a keyboard. The vat hissed open, spilling its grotesque contents onto the floor. An ethereal hand floated beside him, delivering surgical tools to his grasp. In moments, he severed the hand from the vat's occupant and grafted it onto Drake's wrist. Covering the wound with the same white glow, the flesh knitted together seamlessly. Drake's new hand twitched and curled.

"Ah, not quite ready yet,"
Timothy mused.

"Your yolk clings to this shell. Let's see if feeding you will solve that problem. Otherwise, I can always rip your soul out and use another host to see if they can break the lock."

Walking away from Drake's body Timothy holds his own mouth, putting his fingers down his throat to rip the man's name out.

"Dam Al'mon, even millennium later and your still a thorn in my side. Why the master see's you so interesting, I'll never know. But when I bring him back his pets, I will be by his side like I've always deserved."

Twisting his fingers, Timothy carved the number,

'11',

onto Drake's neck. With the aid of the ethereal hands, he lifted Drake's limp body from the table and carried it through a hidden cobblestone tunnel. The dark crimson and ebony-gray bricks glistened under flickering lights. Small inscriptions lined the walls, their meanings lost to time. The tunnel opened into a massive chamber with a sandy pit. Timothy dropped Drake unceremoniously into the pit, the impact kicking up a cloud of dust.

"Now awaken, my Leviathan!"
Timothy declared, snapping a small disk in half. Bright green liquid dripped from its center, pooling over Drake's mouth. As the liquid trickled down his throat, Drake's eyes shot open.

"AAAAAAAHHHHHHHHH!!!"
Drake roared, leaping to his feet. He sprang toward
the pit's edge, clearing 30 feet with ease, but fell
just short from its ledge. Landing on all fours, he
prowled like a wild animal, growling and barking.

Timothy blushed, bringing a trembling hand to his
face as he watched Drake with rapturous delight.

"Oh, my dear son, you're even more magnificent
than I imagined. But be patient; your meal will
come soon. My brood failed at bringing me your
brothers brain to feed to you. But I'm sure your
meal will come to you without my need for
intervention."

Timothy turned, addressing the room as if
speaking to an unseen audience.
"I must bid you adieu, my dear child. Others await
my surgical wonders—a young girl in need of a
heart, a boy requiring a new spine. Mortals are such
fragile creatures. Five thousand years, and they still
toil in the sludge of their weaknesses, wasting what
little they're given."

Raising his withered hands, Timothy's flesh hung in
shreds, pieces dropping like dried leaves. His voice
reverberated with fanaticism.

"I will cleanse this world of parasites. No longer will
they desecrate what was meant to thrive. Long live
the watchful blue flame. Soon, the true master of
undeath shall walk among us again."

As Timothy exited, a colossal wooden and steel door creaked open behind Drake. The beast within roared and charged, smashing through the door in an explosion of splinters and iron shards. Drake emerged into a cheering arena; his monstrous form illuminated by flickering neon lights.

Hovering on a disk, a flamboyant announcer with neon-green hair and ram's horns addressed the crowd. His skintight plastic suit squeaked with every exaggerated gesture.

"[What a night, my horned assembly! LADIES AND GENTLEMEN, ARE YOU READY FOR THE FEAST OF THE BEAST?!]"

The crowd roared, their energy electrifying the air.

"[We've seen him conquer two Iron Jaw Wildebeests Pups! But now, let's see how our Mountain Leviathan handles their MOTHER!]"

A door on the far side of the arena groaned open. The ground trembled as a 20-foot-tall beast lumbered into view. Its iron-jaws snapped menacingly, and its primal roar sent shockwaves through the stands.
Drake's feral eyes locked onto the beast. Without hesitation, he dug his feet into the sand and sprinted forward. Covering the distance in mere seconds, he leapt onto the beasts back, his hands tearing through its flesh. Blood sprayed as chunks of meat fell to the ground.

The beast bucked wildly, but Drake drove it to the ground with a powerful kick to the back of its skull. Standing atop its chest, he roared triumphantly, his mouth dripping with blood and gore. The crowd erupted in frenzied applause.

"[BEHOLD THE POWER OF THE MOUNTAIN LEVIATHAN!]"

"[AND THIS IS ONLY HIS MORTAL FORM FOLKS!]"

Chapter 16
Ethan

"[Bodies litter the battlefield, and none can stand anywhere close to our champion! We are almost ready for the main event of our Blood Moon Harvest Ritual. Now, everyone, get ready for the feast of meats—watch the waterworks!]"

Bars suspended above the battle ring jittered to life, releasing a torrent of blood from their sprinklers onto the arena and its roaring audience. The crowd erupted in chaotic cheers, their hands snapping and clawing at the crimson rain. Amidst the cacophony, the announcer danced atop his hover disk, his garish neon clothes squeaking with every exaggerated move, reveling in the chaos below.

But something shifted. Drake—now an unrecognizable beast—paused, sniffing the air. His sharp, shark-like jaw opened slightly as he turned his attention skyward. His chocolate eyes, one of the few remnants of his former self, flickered with something beyond instinct.

The announcer noticed.
"[What is it, Leviathan? Is it not enough for you?]"

He laughed, the crowd joining in mockery.

In the shadows of the rafters, Ethan moved silently, placing small devices on the bars. His bruised and battered form blended into the darkness, but he couldn't avoid Drake's heightened senses. The beasts tentacles shot out, missing him by mere inches as Ethan darted out of reach.

The announcer's gaze followed Drake's, narrowing. He snapped his fingers, and a surge of purple energy yanked Ethan from the shadows. Bound by glowing tendrils, Ethan dangled helplessly above the ring.

"[What do we have here?]"
The announcer jeered, dragging Ethan closer for all to see.

"[The miracle rat still survives!]"

Boos and jeers erupted from the crowd, a cacophony of disdain.

"That's right!"
The announcer spun Ethan around like a trophy.

"[This rat thinks himself worthy to walk among the transcended!]"

"MONSTERS!"
Ethan's voice rang out over the mic, defiant and unyielding.

The announcer leaned closer, his sharp open mouth grin widening.
"[What was that, rat?]"

Ethan spat in his mouth, his voice rising so all could hear.
"[I SAID MONSTERS! All of you!]"

The announcer recoiled, as he attempted to vomit.
The crowd gasped and howled; their rage palpable.
Ethan seized the moment, his voice booming
through the stolen microphone.

"[I don't know who or what you all think you are,
but you're monsters! You're no better than Splicer
junkies—manipulating your bodies and thinking it
makes you superior! You pit brothers against each
other for money, and you actually believe in the
fantasies written by some deranged child. You're
egotistical, self-righteous—]"

The announcer slammed him to the ground,
cutting him off mid-rant. Ethan gasped for air, pain
searing through his chest as the crowd erupted in
laughter.

"[You want it, boy?]"
The announcer taunted.

"[Do you all want to see the dog eat the rat?]"

"YES!"
The crowd thundered.

"[Well, you have it folks! Let's watch the dog feast
on the pitiful rat!]"

The announcer flung Ethan across the arena,
slamming him into the blood-soaked area walls.
Ethan barely managed to raise his shield in time to
deflect the worst of the impact, but Drake was
already charging.
                                    "Wait, Drake!"
Ethan shouted, diving to the side just in time to
avoid a swipe of Drake's claws. He rolled to his feet,
firing his grappling hook into Drake's chest.

Pg.176

"I-I-I don't want to hurt you Drake!"
Ethan retracted the hook to yank himself toward
his brother.

With his robotic arm, he punched Drake square in
the jaw, releasing a burst of electricity. The monster
roared in pain but remained unfazed. Spinning,
Drakes tail whipped Ethan into the sand. Ethan
coughed up blood, barely managing to dodge as
Drake pounced, claws sinking into the ground
where he'd been seconds before.

Tears streamed down as he raised his trembling
hand. "What did they do to you, Drake? Please, talk
to me!"

Drake roared; his once-human features now
distorted by the monstrous transformation. His
body had grown to over twelve feet in length, and
his skin was now a dark gray leather, with patches
of coarse hair that covered his head & chest.
Several long white spikes dressed his back like that
of a porcupine, and a thick lizard like tail had
sprouted from Drake's backside, it's tip bladed. His
elongated limbs & fingers were covered in a matted
dark metal, and his shark-like jaw contained a
multitude of metallic fangs.

Desperation took hold. Ethan dropped smoke
bombs as he ran, filling the ring with a thick haze.
"Drake, please! I-I-I-I I'm your- your- your
brother!"

From above, the announcer waved his hand.
"Let's not keep our audience waiting!"

"[Don't worry folks!]"
the announcer declared.

"[I'll clear this up!]"

Pg.177

As he dissipated the smoke with a wave of his hand, Ethan seized the moment. Firing his grappling hook it wrapped around the announcer's leg.

"What the—"
the announcer yelled, but before he could react, Drake rushed past, dragging the cord and slamming the announcer into the ground.

Turning around, Drake pounced back landing on him. Crushing his spine, Drake took no time to rip and swallow his head, not stopping there.

The crowd cheered in an uproar.

Ethan held his mouth as he tried not to vomit, doing so he didn't notice as a hidden tentacle shot out from Drake's side, punching Ethan in the face. Slamming him down, it grappled Ethan with its unmeasurable strength.

Drake charged, launching more tentacles to pin Ethan to the ground. Though for Ethan just the one could hold him down. The others just continued to press, crushing several of Ethan's ribs in the process.

"Stop!"
Ethan's desperation broke his voice.

The gem in the pointer knuckle of Ethan's robotic fist glowed pink, releasing a bead of energy that struck Drake's head. The beast paused, his claws hovering just inches from Ethan's face.

"Pa- Pa- Please... let me go!"

Drake hesitated, the glow in his eyes dimming. However, Drake just continued to lean, his claws just inches from Ethan's face.

Pg.178

Ethan gritted his teeth, looking at the glow in the pink gem on his prosthetic hand's pointer finger. It mirrored the glow in Drake's eyes. "{Single-word commands... ARE YOU KIDDING ME THAT'S LAME!}"

Quickly Ethan yelled out again, "Drop!"

Drake complied; another bead of pink energy struck his head.

"{I guess Mr. War Mage was right with their limitations, but I can make this work.}"

The crowd roared in anger, throwing objects into the pit. One struck Drake, breaking his trance. With a guttural snarl, he lunged at Ethan again.

Ethan barely dodged, his robotic arm sparking against Drake's claws as he blocked the attack with his shield. Pain shot through his body as Drake's tail swung around whipping Ethan across the ring.

"Drake, plea- plea- please! It's me—your brother!" Ethan's breathing labored from the crushed ribs.

For a moment, Drake froze, his monstrous form trembling. Then, his mouth opened, and a garbled sound escaped:
"...E-Ethan..."

Tears streamed down Ethan's face. "Yes it's me! Fight it Drake!"

Drake's claws faltered, but a purple glow formed in his eyes. Drake roared with renewed fury as Ethan braced himself for the impact, but he couldn't feel his body. Drake struck at him with his devastating claws, launching Ethan into the air.

Ethan's mind raced on why Drake didn't just slaughter him with that single strike. "{That should have killed me. What's going on!}"

Drake grabbed the ground beneath himself, his mouth opening to manifest a gigantic ball of necrotic energy. Regaining control of his body, Ethan yelled out for him to stop, but the pink gem in his fist didn't glow this time, only the green gem in his pinky knuckle.

"{Oh come on!!}"

"{WORK DAMN YOU!}"

Falling, Ethan pushed his robotic fist outward as Drake launched the ball of necrotic energy. Over and over again he pushed out his fist, yelling for the blast to stop but it wouldn't. Just then, as the ball struck his palm, another gem in his middle finger's knuckle glowed a bright white light. Forming a shield around Ethan's body. The ball became sporadic, mixing with the Necrotic Energy. In an instant the shield burst, launching massive black & white disks into the devil audience. Gently brought back down by one of the disks, Ethan called out to Drake one more time.

"COME ON!! DRAKE, PLEASE LISTEN TO ME!!"
But Ethan's desperate yell was drowned out by the thunderous cheers of the crowd, who chanted Drake's name as if he were a deity.

Drake stood motionless for a moment, his monstrous Leviathan form towering above the battlefield. Voices screamed in his head, urging him to kill, to consume, to dominate. But faintly, like a whisper through a storm, he heard something else:

"I'm sorry, Drake... I love you."

The whisper pulled at the edges of his fractured mind, a flicker of who he used to be, fought against the darkness.

Ethan, on the other hand, clenched his fists, determination radiating from his trembling form. He wasn't just fighting for Drake—he was fighting for every piece of good they still had left. For Kat. For the people who couldn't fight back. For the little boy who once believed in heroes.

"I-I-I won't lose you again,"
Ethan whispered to Drake.

Realizing his voice alone couldn't reach his brother, Ethan frantically reached into his backpack, pulling out another small jar of robotic ants. He hesitated for a moment.

"{I was hoping I wouldn't have to use these... but you have left me no other choice Drake. I hope this can knock some sense into you.}"

Reloading his grappling hook, Ethan charged toward the hulking figure of Drake. The crowd roared as Drake let out a deafening bellow, his tentacles lashing out like whips. Ethan dove, narrowly avoiding the strikes. Drake lunged forward; his massive claws aimed directly at Ethan. Just as they were about to collide, Ethan leapt into the air.

Drake tried to rear back and impale him, but Ethan planted his robotic hand against the spikes, sparks flying as the hand dragged across their surfaces. Spinning mid-air, he fired his grappling hook at the metal pipes above the arena. As the hook retracted, Ethan soared through the air, corking the jar and pouring its contents onto Drake's back.

The robotic ants scurried into the folds of Drake's mutilated flesh, latching on and exploding in quick succession. Smoke engulfed Drake's massive form as the crowd leaned forward in anticipation.

Ethan landed on the ground and shouted, his voice breaking with emotion, "Her- Her- Her name was Kat! She- she never made fun of the way I spoke—she reminded me of u- u-you! She was tough, she lifted me up when I-I-I was falling apart, just like you u-u-u used to!"

Tears streamed down Ethan's face as he continued. "She believed in me... Drake... even when I-I-I-I didn't believe in my- my-my- myself. We fought to help people, not for money, ba- ba-ba but for something bigger. And then I-I-I lost her because I-I-I was stupid. Just like I almost lost you... again."

As the smoke cleared, Drake stood unharmed, but the glow in his eyes faded and for a moment his dark chocolate eyes returned. The crowd erupted in a frenzy as Drake stampeded toward his brother.

Ethan fell to his knees, lowering his head, " I-I-I I'm sorry... Drake. I-I-I I've been such a coward. You've always been stronger than me... Please, just make it quick."

Drake roared, his tentacles shooting forward to wrap around Ethan. But instead of striking him down, they yanked Ethan into Drake's massive arms.
Through the haze of cheers and chaos, Ethan heard a familiar voice.

"I'd never make this hug quick,"

"DRAKE!"
Ethan cried, clutching his brother as tightly as he could.

"It's me, little man."
Tears streamed down Drake's face as he held Ethan close.

"I'm sorry I couldn't fight it sooner."

The two brothers sobbed, their reunion silencing everything else in the world.

After a long moment, Ethan pulled back, his voice trembling.
"How- how- how are you... you again-?"

"I don't know. I just heard your voice. It cut through all the noise. Thank you little man."

Ethan scoffed through his tears. "Yea-yea-yea yeah, right. I-I-I thought you were about to rip me to shreds."
"I was,"
Drake admitted.

"But after I... ate the announcer, I started to feel like myself again. The more I consumed, the less the fog controlled me."

Ethan gagged.
"That's disgusting... Wait-wait-wait, does that mean you were yourself when-when-when you shot magic at me?!"
Drake's eyes darted away.
"Uh... no."

Ethan punched him in the shoulder, then winced as his hand throbbed.
"You're such a jerk!"

Drake laughed, as he punched Ethan's shoulder as well, however Drake's light punch sent Ethan flying.
"Fancy new-"

"ETHAN!!"
Rushing Drake caught him with two of his tentacles.

"OW, WHAT THE FUCK!"

Drake laughed, as he set Ethan down,
"Sorry, guess I don't know my own monster strength. I like the new arm, shame you had to lose the old one. I hope there's a badass story behind it."

"Damn right there is,"
Ethan smirked.

"I turned that older devil to *ASH*! And I stole their tech. Now I can cast magic."
Ethan raised his robotic arm in a flex, his face extraordinarily smug.

"REALLY?!"
Drake's face lit up.

"LEGENDARY, little man!"

"Why- why- why do you sound surprised?"
Ethan shot back, side-eyeing him.

Before Drake could respond, the air around them grew heavy. A necrotic ray streaked through the arena, narrowly missing Ethan.

"NO WORM COULD KILL ME!"

The older devil's voice boomed as he emerged from the shadows, his body crackling with dark energy. His untouched form flawless as if it had never been hurt. His glowing runes pulsed with malevolent power.

Ethan froze, his eyes widening.
"How-how-how are you still alive?! I-I-I turned u-u-u-u-you into ash!"

The devil smirked, launching another necrotic ray. "Magic you foolish boy. Let me teach you one last lesson."

Drake intercepted the beam with his tentacle, roaring in pain but shielding Ethan.
"Run Ethan! Find your Dad! You're going to have to do it without me!"

"I-I-I I'm not leaving you again! We fight together, or... not at all. You've got my back, and I-I-I I've got yours."

Drake stared at his brother, seeing not the scared little boy he had left behind, but a capable, fearless man. He smirked.
"Alright, but if you die, I'll bring you back just to kill you myself."

"Same to you, old man."

The two brothers turned to face the devil; their resolve unshakable. Ethan pulled out another jar of robotic ants, and Drake readied his claws.

The devil laughed.
"How sweet. You two really think you have a chance."

Ethan pointed at him, fire in his eyes.
"Big talk from a burnt chicken nugget."

The devil snarled, flames erupting from his mouth and hands.

Drake laughed as he cracked his knuckles.
"Come on punk. I'm going to enjoy this!"

The brothers roared in unison, charging at the devil in a blinding wave of green, blue, and yellow.

Epilogue
Benny

An explosion of colors rained across the monitors, illuminating the horrors unfolding on every screen. Ethan and Drake fought valiantly against the devil, their combined efforts nearly overpowering him. But the tide shifted as more devils joined the fray, swarming them like a dark tide.

The onslaught separated the brothers. Ethan was dragged away, his screams muffled by the cultists surrounding him. Drake, restrained by glowing chains, roared in anguish as they locked him down. The cultists, robed in crimson and black, chanted in unison. One by one, they drew their sacrificial blades, each glowing with pulsating runes. The serrated edges gleamed, dripping with unholy intent.

Drake's voice cracked as he screamed, "[ETHAN! NO!]" His muscles bulged against the chains, veins popping along his arms and neck as he fought with every ounce of strength, but he couldn't move.

The cultists descended upon Ethan, plunging their blades into him. Blood sprayed across the sandy floor, pooling beneath his body as his cries grew weaker. They dragged his lifeless form toward the wall. With a guttural chant, the wall twisted and split, forming a grotesque doorway of flesh and stone. Without hesitation, they tossed Ethan's limp green glowing body into the darkness beyond.

Pg.187

"[BRING HIM BACK!]"
Drake's voice was raw, his throat torn from screaming. But the cultists ignored him. The doorway sealed shut, leaving only silence.

Most of the monitors showed different angles of the carnage. On one, Anthony was carried off alone by members of the horned crown cult, his bloodied face barely recognizable. Another showed Lincoln stumbling through a labyrinth, an adult Iron Jaw Wildebeest chasing him relentlessly. And on yet another, Felicity wept uncontrollably, her elegant crimson and gold dress soaked in Baillie's blood. She cradled her lifeless body in a darkened room, her cries echoing in the void.

"Do you see what I told you earlier Benjamin?"
A voice rasped behind him, low and menacing.

"We mortals are weak, and these... these few are no exception."

Benny squirmed in the chair, but the bindings held him firm. His eyes, forced open by cruel metal forceps, stung from the monitors' flickering light. A clawed hand rested heavily on his shoulder, its nails biting into his skin.

"Why... why are you doing this to them?"
Benny's voice cracked with desperation.

"Because they are the Heavenly Chosen Few,"
The creature whispered, its voice like dry leaves scraping against stone.

"And they must be punished for what they did."

A clawed finger traced down Benny's cheek, slicing it open. Blood welled and dripped down as the creature leaned closer, its tongue slithering out to lap at the wound. The grotesque sound of slurping filled the darkness.

"What... what are you talking about?"
Benny's voice trembled.

"Heavenly Chosen Few? What does that even mean?"

"They are the ones reborn from the Purge Point Benjamin. Their shells were given to them by Lord Al'mon. It took five millennia to find them, to test them, to make them, and here they are—ripe for redemption."

"I don't understand!"
Benny struggled against the restraints.

"Please... just let me go!"

The creature's laughter filled the air, a sound that made Benny's blood turn cold.
"Oh, oh, oh you must not go just yet.

"Why?!"

"You will understand soon enough. You are important too Benjamin. You are the one that gazes through all voids. Watching the Threads of Fate bind us all and noting it down for history to be. Without you we wouldn't be able to even commence the ritual."

"What?"
Benny's voice was a whisper, barely audible over the devil's words.

"You are the eternal scribe, destined to bear witness to the unraveling of a foolish man's sins. Through your eyes, the annals of history will be rewritten—for the glory of the All-Mighty Creator."

"No! Please, stop this!" Benny's cries were swallowed by the darkness as the clawed hand tightened around his neck.

The creature leaned closer against Benny's ear. "Tonight Benjamin, you will see everything. And through your eyes, the Creator's wrath shall be known.

"NOW, do take note Young Metatromis! HAHAHAHA!"

The monitors flickered, leaving Benny alone with the sound of his own terrified breathing and the devil's laughter echoing into the void at the sight of those he knew were to be slaughtered like lambs.

Or were they?

To Be Continued...
In Devil's Harvest; Fate's Bonds

Short Story & Thanks

I wrote this book for you—after **years of trials and burnt-out dreams**. For so long, I pushed hard but never followed through, leaving so many creations unfinished. My entire life felt like a string of *abandoned sparks*, flickering out before they could ignite. But **not anymore**.

Things have changed—**I've changed**. My will and passion can no longer keep this story locked away. So, thank you. Not just for picking up this book, but for **opening it and making it this far**. Your support helps *Purple Mage Publishing* push forward, turning more dreams into reality.

I'm done *running blind with flares in my eyes*. I want to give the world not just this story, but **many more**. And if you've made it here, I invite you to *jump through the purple portal with me*. On the other side, you'll find my **socials, other creations, and the incredible work** of our talented freelancers—crafted just for you.

Jump Through the Purple Portal:
https://linktr.ee/purple_Mage_Publishing

Special Thanks to the **Decay family & friends**—the true *purple gate guards*. Your unwavering support helped me make it here, to finally **share the beauty beyond the gate**.